Who Needs a Duke

FATED FOR A ROGUE BOOK 5

WAYWARD DUKES
BOOK NINE

AMANDA MARIEL

This is a work of fiction. Names, characters, organizations, places, events, and incidents are either products of the author's imagination or are used fictitiously.

Published by Brook Ridge Press

Also by Amanda Mariel

Ladies and Scoundrels series

Scandalous Endeavors

Scandalous Intentions

Scandalous Redemption

Scandalous Wallflower

Scandalous Liaison

Dancing with Serendipity

Fabled Love Series

Enchanted by the Earl

Captivated by the Captain

Enticed by Lady Elianna

Delighted by the Duke

Lady Archer's Creed series

Amanda Mariel writing with Christina McKnight

Theodora

Georgina

Adeline

Josephine

Scandal Meets Love series

Love Only Me

Find Me Love

If it's Love

Odd's of Love

Believe in Love

Chance of Love

Love and Holly

Love and Mistletoe

A Rogue's Kiss Series

Her Perfect Rogue

His Perfect Hellion

This Rogue of Mine

Her Perfect Scoundrel

Standalone titles

One Moonlit Tryst

One Enchanting Kiss

Christmas in the Duke's Embrace

One Wicked Christmas

A Lyon in Her Bed (The Lyon's Den connected world)

Courting Temptation (House of Devon connected world)

Forever My Rogue (Love Be a Lady's Charm Connected World)

Wicked Earls' Club

Titles by Amanda Mariel

Earl of Grayson

Earl of Edgemore

Earl of Persuasion

Earl of Stone (Fated for a Rogue)

Fated for a Rogue

A Wallflower's Folly

One Fateful May Day

Fate Gave Me a Duke

Earl of Stone (Wicked Earls' Club)

Who Needs a Duke

Rogue for the Taking

Connected by a Kiss

These are designed so they can standalone

How to Kiss a Rogue (Amanda Mariel)

A Kiss at Christmastide (Christina McKnight)

A Wallflower's Christmas Kiss (Dawn Brower)

Stealing a Rogue's Kiss (Amanda Mariel)

A Gypsy's Christmas kiss (Dawn Brower)

A Duke's Christmas Kiss (Tammy Andresen)

Box sets and anthologies

Visit www.amandamariel.com to see Amanda's current offerings.

One

London, England

"This is going to be your season," Olivia, the Duchess of Thorne, said as she slid one ivory stick from the spillikin pile on the table between them.

Lady Catherine Breckenridge forced a weak smile in response. "Elizabeth is the diamond," Catherine said, then averted her gaze to the ivory sticks.

Catherine's older sister Louisa had married last year. And though her younger sister Elizabeth was of an age, everyone's focus turned to Catherine as the oldest unwed sister. A pity, as she did not wish to marry.

"You shine just as bright." Olivia turned to her husband, William Duke of Thorne who was Catherine's guardian and brother. He was engaged in a card game with their brother Tristen at a nearby table. "Tell her it is true, William."

William turned his attention to Catherine as he tossed a card into the center of the table. "Indeed, and as you are nearing two and twenty, the time has come for you to choose a suitor."

"Though I am quite certain Elizabeth will marry this season, too," Olivia said, then gave Elizabeth a smile. "She was a grand success last year."

"If you call rejecting five proposals a grand success," Tristen said.

"Drat!" Elizabeth exclaimed as the spillikin stick she was attempting to pull out disturbed those around it. She released the stick, then peered at Tristen. "They were ill suited, as you well know."

"The only thing I am aware of is that you, sister, are far too picky."

"Would you have me marry a lord whose interest lays as much in my dowery as my person? Or a scoundrel who will spend his nights at the gaming tables instead of by my side? Perhaps I should have accepted the widower with five children?"

"There was nothing wrong with Lord

Granthum." Tristen tossed a card into the center of the table while Elizabeth tossed a spillikin stick at Tristin.

Catherine watched her siblings bicker with each other, feeling a pang of envy for their carefree banter. As the middle daughter, she had always been the quiet one, content to let her sisters and brothers take the spotlight. But now, as the pressure to marry mounted, Catherine found herself more and more anxious. Perhaps the time had come for her to be more assertive?

"I do not wish to marry," she blurted out, surprising even herself. Silence filled the room as everyone turned to her.

"What do you mean?" William asked, his brow furrowed. "You are the daughter of a duke and sister to myself, the current duke of Thorne. Of course you will marry."

Catherine shook her head. "I do not wish to marry," she said, a strange sense of relief wrapping around her at having voiced her true thoughts. She averted her gaze to the window and focused on the tendrils of rain streaking down the glass. "I don't want to be beholden to a man for the rest of my life simply because it is expected of me. I want to live on my own terms. Do the things that please me without needing permission. I wish to control my own life."

After a moment of shock, Olivia laughed out loud. "Catherine, you jest," she said, shaking her head. "You must believe there is a gentleman out there for you. One that will sweep you off your feet and eradicate any reservations you have regarding marriage."

"I doubt that very much." Catherine reached for another ivory stick, though her mind was no longer on the game.

"I vow you will," Olivia said, a smile in her tone as she turned her attention to William. "You have not fallen in love yet, but you will."

William grinned at his wife. "Save heart, sister, for Olivia is right."

Catherine sighed, not at all surprised by what William and Olivia were saying. They did not understand her plight. She had no wish to be a gentleman's arm piece, and even less of a desire to be his breeding stock. Love was rare among their set, and even with love, men expected much of their wives, including obedience. A wife was a possession. The property of her husband.

She had no wish to be dictated to. No wish to give up her pursuits at a man's whim. What of her work at the orphanage? Or her educational pursuits? What gentleman would allow his wife to spend time with orphans? To teach them?

"But what if I do not wish to fall in love?" Catherine said, her voice low. "What if I simply want to be by myself, without someone else always by my side?"

Tristen snorted. "Then you are a fool, Catherine," he said, shaking his head. "A woman without a husband is worth nothing among the peerage, and you know it as well as I do."

Catherine resisted the urge to argue with her brother. Doing so would not change his mind. Instead, she focused on the game of spillikins, trying to distract herself from the surrounding conversation.

But no matter how many times she won or lost, there was no ignoring the sense of unease that had settled in the pit of her stomach. Olivia and William would not allow her to avoid the season, no matter how much she wished to.

As if he had read her mind, William said, "Regardless, the first ball of the season is less than a fortnight away. You will attend with the rest of us."

"Very well," Catherine conceded.

As the current game came to a close, she stood,

then excused herself, citing a headache. Ignoring Elizabeth's worried glance, she hurried out of the room in search of the solace she would find in the quiet of her own chambers.

Shadows danced across her floor as she paced around the room, trying to escape the weight of her circumstances. She couldn't bear the thought of being forced to marry, to have to spend the rest of her days being subservient to a man. But that was what was expected of her. Could she truly avoid it?

No.

Maybe.

Yes!

She craved more and she would achieve it. There was nothing else for her. She had to maintain her independence. But how?

She paused beside the window and looked out into the night sky, hoping for divine intervention to illuminate her path. A flash of lightening greeted her.

A moment later, a loud knock sounded on the door. "May I come in?" Elizabeth asked softly as she peeked around the edge of the door.

Catherine nodded, and Elizabeth stepped inside, closing the door behind her. They were as close as any sisters could be, but Catherine couldn't help feeling a pang of jealousy for her sister's contentment. Elizabeth was the sort of lady society valued, and would no doubt find the love she sought. More importantly, Elizabeth wished to marry. She wanted to be a wife and mistress of her own home. She desired children of her own and thrived in society's spotlight. Indeed, Elizabeth would make the perfect society wife and enjoy every moment of her duties.

Catherine wished she could be more like Elizabeth. Life would be less complicated if she accepted the role expected of her, but she could not. She was not like Elizabeth and there was no changing that.

"You do not have a headache. Tell me what is really troubling you? Is it the coming season?" Elizabeth asked, concern etched into her features.

Catherine sank onto the edge of her bed. "It is the pressure to marry. The fact I know Olivia and William will not stop encouraging me to find a husband and if I refuse, I will be disappointing them. They mean well, but I cannot do as they wish simply because they think it is best."

Elizabeth sat beside Catherine, taking her sister's hand in hers. "I understand why you wish to remain unwed. Honestly, it would be easier if you felt differently. But I understand why you cannot let our family's expectations dictate your life. You must do what is best for you, because you are the one who has to live with your choices." She met Catherine's gaze, then added. "Know that I support you in whatever you do."

Catherine nodded, grateful for her sister's words of comfort. "I do not want to disappoint them. However, I cannot imagine spending my life under a man's control... not even one I love. Or worse, being forced to bear children while ignoring all of those abandoned in orphanages. I could not live with myself."

"I understand, Catherine," Elizabeth said, squeezing her hand. "Truly, I do."

Elizabeth was the only one save for Catherine's maid that knew of her work at the orphanage. Catherine had tried to speak to William once about the cause and about the children. As a result, he'd forbid her from going back to the orphanage. He had reminded her that lady's help by donating items along with their husbands' money, not by acting as servants and teachers. Then he had forced her to agree to stay away from the orphanage, but she'd continued her work in secret.

Elizabeth squeezed her hand. "You must remember that love and marriage are not always mutually exclusive. A gentleman exists who would support your pursuits and allow you to live a life of your own choosing because he loves you and cannot imagine his life without you."

Catherine sighed, knowing her sister's words held some truth. But finding a gentleman who would love her and support her endeavors had to be more difficult than finding a needle in a haystack.

"Do you truly believe that?" she asked, a hint of desperation in her voice. "Is it possible for me to find a husband who will not restrain me when my wishes are so unconventional?"

"I believe it is with my whole heart, Catherine. So enjoy the season. The worst thing that can happen is you remain unwed at season's end, or fall madly in love with the perfect gentleman for you." She smiled. "Either way, you win."

Catherine sighed, she couldn't imagine a future where she could continue to follow her passions, as well as have a husband who supported her endeavors.

As if sensing her doubts, Elizabeth squeezed her hand once more. "Do not worry, Catherine. You are a strong, intelligent woman. You will be alright no matter what path life carries you down."

Though her sister's words were comforting, she still felt a sense of unease. She would have to navigate the social expectations of the *ton* with care. But she was determined to do so with her head held high and her independence intact.

With a deep breath, Catherine rose from the bed and straightened her gown. "Thank you, Elizabeth. The hour grows late. Stop fretting over me and take yourself to bed." She bumped her shoulder playfully against her sisters.

Elizabeth smiled as she stood up. "Indeed. But please remember, I am always here for you. No matter what." She gave Catherine a hug before leaving the room.

Catherine watched as her sister left, gratitude for the love and support of her sister improving her mood. She would have to face the season head on, but she also knew she had the strength and determination to do so.

With a sense of purpose, Catherine walked over to her writing desk and penned a letter to the orphanage. She would not let the pressures of society keep her from helping those in need.

As she wrote, the sound of the quill scratching against the paper was the only noise in the room. But in Catherine's mind, she could hear her own voice, strong and unwavering, as she vowed to keep her independence, no matter where it may lead her.

Two

Charles De Vere, Duke of Bedford, dreaded the coming season. He enjoyed women and drink as well as the next man, but abhorred innocent misses—and worse—their mamas. One would think his reputation would be enough to keep them at bay. Unfortunately, they were all too happy to look past his debauchery in order to capture his fortune and title.

As he looked out over the rolling hills of his estate, he knew he needed to appear at the season's events. His station demanded as much. Besides, it would give him an opportunity to escape the monotony of his daily routine.

He dropped into an armchair near the hearth, a glass of brandy in one hand and an invitation to the first ball of the season in his other. Resigned to his fate, he read the scrolled handwriting, then took a deep drink of brandy, relishing the way it warmed his throat. As there would be no escaping the season, he might as well start with this ball.

But then, he did not have to accept every invitation that came his way.

Charles tapped the crystal glass with his index finger. The sound echoed through the study as he contemplated his predicament. Attending the ball would not be such a distasteful idea if it did not come with the attentions of husband hunting mamas and their title grabbing daughters. It was the marriage mart business that made the entire ordeal unbearable.

He took a drink, tilted his head back, and swirled the amber liquid around in his mouth before swallowing. Bloody hell. He was tired of being chased like a wild stallion. He would not allow the *tons* unwed daughters and their title hunting mamas to ruin his good time.

This season, he would avoid their pursuits.

He held the invitation out toward a footman and said, "Send my acceptance."

"At once, Your Grace." The footman took the parchment before offering a bow.

As the footman left the room, Charles leaned back in his chair with a sigh. Avoiding the debutantes and their mothers would not be an easy feat, but he was determined to do so. He had come much too close to being caught in the traps of title-grabbing debutantes the previous season. Avoiding the marriage trap had become exhausting, and as the season wore on the marriage minded misses and their mama's only grew more creative. He needed a protection of sorts, a shield against their machinations if he were to enjoy this season.

He took another sip of his brandy, relishing the way it burned down his throat. He would need to come up with a plan, something foolproof that would allow him to enjoy the season with no unwanted entanglements.

Charles sat there, lost in thought, until the sound of horse's hooves on the cobblestone drive brought him back to reality. He stood up from his chair, setting his tumbler on the table beside it, and walked to the window to see who had arrived.

To his surprise, it was his long-time friend and fellow rake, Lord Tristin Breckenridge. Charles grinned, looking forward to the distraction.

Once inside, Tristen accepted a brandy. He leaned against the mantlepiece as he took a deep drink. "You are blessed to be without sisters, and let me tell you how glad I am to be a younger son. I would not wish to be William," Tristen vented. "But never mind that." He waved a dismissive hand before taking another gulp of his brandy.

Charles chuckled, gesturing for Tristin to continue. "I could use the distraction, so tell me the whole sordid tale."

Tristen rolled his eyes. "William and Olivia are trying to get Catherine to marry, pressuring her to find a suitor. As her guardians, they are right to do so, but listening to their exchanges grows tedious."

Charles took a drink from his own glass. "And what about Catherine? Has she no wish to marry?"

Tristen shook his head. "Of course she doesn't, for if she did, there would be nothing to bicker about. Contrary to her temperament, she blurted out in front of the whole family that she has no wish to marry, though I cannot imagine why. She is a duke's daughter, for Heaven's sake. What else is there for her?"

"What else indeed?" Charles frowned, feeling a sense of sympathy for Catherine. He understood all too well the suffocating feeling of being trapped by society's expectations and the pressure to conform.

"Regardless, her mind will not be swayed. It is

bound to make for a turbulent season. Olivia and William have already made it clear Catherine will attend society events and is expected to search for a husband."

"I can sympathize with her," Charles said, then took a drink, nearly choking on the brandy when he realized Catherine could be the answer to his own problem. He recovered before adding, "After all, have we not been avoiding the same trap?"

"Indeed, but we are not ladies."

"True." Charles raised a dark brow. "Perhaps she will change her mind."

"I daresay she had better, but I am not certain she will. She seems quite determined to become an old maid and is already well on her way."

Charles swirled the liquor in his tumbler, lost in thought. He had met Tristen's sister a handful of times over the years. She was an attractive lady, though quite shy based on what he knew of her. Though, in all honesty, he'd not payed much attention to her. Beyond the fact that she was his friend's sister, she was also an innocent, which made her entirely off limits, as far as he was concerned. "Has she no suitors?" Charles asked.

Tristen chuckled. "Our parlor was overflowing with them last season. Though more than half of them called for Elizabeth, there were half a dozen or more with an eye toward Catherine."

"In that case, I doubt anyone will change her mind."

"Bloody hell. Let us speak of something else." Tristin drained his glass, then sat it on the sideboard. "Better still, let us go find a proper distraction."

The signet ring on Tristin's hand sparkled with his movement catching Charles's eye. It was a symbol of their bond, for he wore a similar one. They were both part of the wayward duke's. A secret group of men who vowed to always help one another in times of need. Could Charles bring Tristin's sister into his escapade when he and Tristin were bound in such a way?

He would not contemplate it now.

"Whites?" Charles suggested, running his finger over the emblem on his own ring.

Tristin shook his head. "To civilized."

"Madam Crimson's then." Charles suggested.

Tristen gave a firm nod, then pivoted toward the door.

If Charles could convince Lady Catherine to pretend to be his betrothed, it would keep the husband hunting mamas at bay, as well as please her family. And so long as he did not compromise the chit, he would not be betraying Tristin and his vow to the wayward duke's.

He knew it was a risky plan, but the thought of being able to enjoy the season free from unwanted attention made it worth considering.

The hell with considering. The plan was perfect. A pretend betrothal would allow them both to get what they wanted. He decided to approach Lady Catherine at his first opportunity.

He climbed into the carriage, then glanced at Tristin. He would be livid when he discovered what Charles had done, but their friendship was strong. Tristin would forgive him in time.

Three

The first ball of the season had arrived and Catherine dutifully attended, with Olivia and William as chaperones and Elizabeth at her side.

Music drifted through the air as Catherine moved through the crowded ballroom, nodding politely at acquaintances and attempting to avoid the prying eyes of the *ton*. But try as she might, Catherine could not escape the unwanted attention. Young men approached her, hoping to catch her eye and secure a dance. Knowing what was expected of her, she accepted their invitations.

As the night wore on, Catherine grew increasingly frustrated. She longed for the night to end. None of the gentleman present suited her, for they all sought proper society wives. She fanned herself as she sighed. She would give nearly anything to be tucked away in her chamber, or at the orphanage teaching the girls to sew or read, rather than here being forced to smile and dance with gentlemen that did not catch her interest.

She moved to a row of chairs, desperate to get a temporary reprieve among the wallflowers. Many of which were her friends.

Before she could sit, the Duke of Bedford approached her, his dark gaze intense as he took her hand. "Lady Catherine," he said in a low voice. "Might I have the honor of this dance?"

For a moment, Catherine was surprised. She had never given much thought to the duke, beyond acknowledging he was a notorious rake and a close friend of her brother Tristin. But then her curiosity got the best of her. He had never paid her any attention before. So why now?

Catherine hesitated for a moment, studying the duke. She could detect a hint of mischief in his dark eyes, but there was also something else. He seemed genuinely interested in her. The very idea should frighten her given his reputation, however, she could not help but be curious. Catherine took his outstretched hand and allowed him to lead her to the dance floor.

As they waltzed, he kept his gaze fixed on her, studying her as if he wished to unearth her deepest secrets. The very idea should terrify her, but somehow it only made her more curious. "Why have you asked me to dance?"

"You are my friend's sister. Why shouldn't I dance with you?"

She noted the determination in his gaze and decided to discover his true motivation. "I do not believe your friendship with Tristin is the reason for this dance."

"Then it is true." He grinned. "You are an intelligent lady."

"What is your true motive?"

"I wish to speak with you," he said, then twirled her out before bringing her close once more. "In private."

"That would be improper, Your Grace."

"Ah, but I am certain you will find it worth your time."

She narrowed her gaze, searching his face. There were no clues to be found, only a strong jawline, straight aristocratic nose, and high cheekbones capped by sleek black hair that curled at his nape.

The duke was a fine specimen of a man. Dark and dangerous, and all too handsome. It was no wonder he collected women like she collected books. "I doubt that I could benefit from time alone with you."

"Oh, but you can," he said as the song ended. He leaned close as he led her back toward Olivia and whispered, "Meet me in the garden in fifteen minutes. You can slip out through the door adjacent to the ladies' retiring room."

Before she had a chance to reply, they had reached Olivia's side.

The duke bowed. "Thank you for the dance, Lady Catherine. It was a pleasure."

She did not know what game she and the duke were playing, but she found it rather amusing and so she followed his lead. Catherine curtsied, a small smile tugging at the corners of her lips. "The pleasure was mine, Your Grace."

She watched him go with a moment's regret. She couldn't help but be drawn in by his charm and charisma. But could she meet him in private? Surely he did not mean to ruin his friend's sister. Even a rogue had principles, and he and Tristen had a long-standing friendship. Besides, everyone knew the duke did not have a penchant for innocent ladies.

What else could he want with her? Was it worth

the risk to find out? If they were discovered together, she would be ruined. Worse, they might be forced to marry regardless of what either of them wanted. A fact that would not have escaped the duke.

As Catherine weighed her options, she noticed the duke exit through the large doors opened to the balcony. In a moment of haste, she turned to Olivia and William, who were engaged in conversation with other guests, and excused herself to go to the retiring room.

She made her way to the heavy oak door the duke had told her to use and slipped out into the cool night air. Her heart pounded with welcome excitement even as she prayed they were not caught.

The garden was quiet, the only sound the music drifting from the ballroom and carrying on the gentle breeze. Moon light cast an ethereal glow over the garden as she strode down the center path, not sure where to find His Grace, the Duke of Bedford.

Before long, she spotted him leaning against a marble statue with his arms folded across his chest. He pushed away from the statue and stood tall as she approached, his gaze locking with hers.

"You came," he said, his voice low.

"I did," Catherine replied, trying to keep her voice from trembling.

"Good." He stepped closer, his gaze roaming over her face. "You have no cause for concern, Lady Catherine."

"Your Grace," she said, stopping in an effort to maintain some distance. "I confess your invitation intrigued me, though I have no wish to linger. Please do not delay. What is it you wished to speak with me about?"

Charles took a step closer, his gaze fixed on hers. "Tristin told me about your declaration not to marry." He took a step closer, and Catherine's heart began to race. "I wanted to see if we might be of assistance to one another." He took another step in her direction.

She felt heat spread through her at his words. How dare Tristin share her wishes? And what was the duke suggesting? Surely he was not propositioning her to be his mistress. She raised a hand up in front of her, palm out, as if to hold him back. "Tristin had no right to speak of my wishes. Furthermore, I will not—"

"Be that as it may, in this instance, you might thank him."

“Why ever would I do that?” She asked, anger lacing her voice.

"Because we have a mutual goal and the ability to help each other. If Tristin had not shared your plight with me, I never would have approached you. However, I am grateful he did, and believe you will be as well once you hear me out.” He paused for a minute, his gaze searching hers. “I want to engage you in a pretend courtship.”

"And I should be grateful for your attentions? Are you daft? If I agreed every gentleman in London would be sure to have renewed interest in me." She lowered her hand to her side, clutching both hands into fists as her anger bubbled back to the surface. "You are a duke! Every man wants whatever seems to interest you. That would not help me in the least.”

"Not if what I want is already spoken for." He smiled.

"Spoken for," she gasped. "I am not spoken for, nor do I wish to be."

"But you desire to be free from unwanted attention, do you not?" The duke took another step toward her, his chest coming dangerously close to hers. "I can help you."

"How?" Catherine asked, studying him warily.

"By pretending you are mine," he said. “Naturally,

the courtship will progress to an engagement. Once we are believed to be engaged your suitors will look elsewhere."

Catherine's heart skipped a beat. Was he truly suggesting they fake a betrothal? The idea was scandalous, but a part of her could not deny the thrill that ran through her at the thought of spending an entire season at his side. She stared up into his eyes, seeing the determination there, and knew he was committed to this course.

"By pretending to be engaged, we will both be removed from the pool of eligible lords and ladies. We will be able to enjoy the season without worrying over unwanted pressures and undesired courtships."

"And when the season is over? Then what?" she asked giving his plan serious consideration. "How do we escape the parsons' noose without causing a scandal?"

He placed his hands on her shoulders and said, "We do not, but your reputation will remain intact."

"How?"

"I will have a public liaison after which you will call off the engagement. No one will blame you." He smiled. "Hell, they will probably applaud you for putting me in my place over my unseemly behavior.

You will be the paragon and I the rogue they all know me to be."

She drew in a deep breath. Averting her gaze to the starlit sky, she considered his proposal. It was risky, scandalous, and could potentially ruin her reputation forever. But being the Duke's fiancée would elevate her status in society. It would provide her with new avenues to help the orphans, in addition to pleasing William and Olivia while keeping unwanted suitors at bay. Besides, she would not be the first lady to jilt a man. If all went according to his plan, everything would end well enough.

"What do you stand to gain?" She asked, skepticism thick in her voice.

He smoothed his cravat. "Same as you, a reprieve from the marriage mart."

She averted her gaze for a moment. "Very well," she said, her voice unwavering despite her remaining reservations. "I will agree to your fake proposal."

A smile spread across the Duke's face, triumph and satisfaction evident in his expression. He leaned in and placed a chaste kiss on her cheek. "You won't regret this, Lady Catherine."

As he pulled away, Catherine felt a shiver run

down her spine. She knew agreeing to his proposal would have consequences, at the least her family would be overset when she jilted the duke, but she could not deny the excitement surging through her. This was the sort of mischief her sister Louisa would have gotten embroiled in before she married. No-one would ever expect it of Catherine. A fact that would make pulling the whole scheme off much easier.

Still, she would have to tread carefully and hope the Duke kept his word.

"We will dance another set this evening and I will call on you in the morning."

Unease crept back into her conscious, and she said, "You have never paid me any attention in the past. What do we tell people who question our motives? How do I explain our sudden fondness for each other to my family?"

"It is fast, but I believe we can manage to convince everyone that we have fallen in love. If they believe we are in love, they will not question our hast in becoming betrothed."

Catherine nodded slowly, taking a deep breath to steady herself. "Indeed, you are right. I will give the performance of a lifetime and expect the same from you."

"I have no doubt you will," the Duke said, a gleam in his eye. "Now, shall we return to the ballroom?"

She nodded, then took a step back.

"Go in the way you came out. I will wait here for a while to avoid raising suspicion."

She nodded then pivoted toward the house.

The duke called after her, "Save the final dance for me."

Four

Charles arrived at The Duke of Thorne's residence during the popular hours for gentlemen to call. He was not surprised to discover several other gentlemen crowded in the parlor near the ladies Catherine and Elizabeth. They were both beautiful women and highborn ladies who had danced nearly every dance at last nights ball. One would be a fool to expect their drawing room to be empty.

A pang of regret stabbed him as he caught sight of Lady Catherine in conversation with Lord Grayling. She was beautiful, her blond curls caught at the back of her head and blue eyes dancing as she smiled at Grayling. The young earl would be a good match for her if she desired marriage. Perhaps she would fall in love with him if Charles did not stand in the way. But as he strode toward her, he pushed those thoughts aside. He had made a promise to Lady Catherine. A promise that would benefit them both.

"My dear Lady Catherine," he said, bowing deeply before her. "You look radiant this morning."

She looked up at him, her eyes widening in surprise. "Your Grace," she said, offering a curtsey. "What brings you here this morning?"

He could not have planned her reaction better. If he did not know of their arrangement, he would believe she'd been genuinely surprised at his arrival. Any doubts he'd harbored about her ability to be convincing disappeared.

He pressed a kiss to her knuckles. "I came to call on you." Charles flashed a charming smile. "Will you do me the honor of joining me for a stroll through the gardens?"

Lady Catherine hesitated for a moment, her gaze flickering toward the other gentlemen in the room. But then she nodded, taking his arm and allowed him to lead her from the house.

The early afternoon air was crisp, the sun just beginning to warm the earth as heavy clouds hung in the sky. Charles glanced at her as they walked, wondering if she had changed her mind about their fake courtship.

Perhaps her surprise had not been an act at all. Maybe she thought he'd been foxed last night and would forget their arrangement after sleeping it off. Or maybe she simply did not trust him enough to continue their game.

Charles led Lady Catherine toward a secluded bench beneath a blooming cherry tree, then took a seat beside her. He inhaled the sweet scent of her perfume, lavender and vanilla, as he searched for something to talk about. His heart beat a little harder as he angled his body toward hers. Still she said nothing.

"I hope you don't mind me saying this, but you seem quite distracted today, Lady Catherine," he said, breaking the silence. "Is something troubling you?"

Lady Catherine's eyes widened for a moment before she composed herself. "Not at all, Your Grace. I am just a little overwhelmed with all the attention I'm receiving."

"I can well imagine," Charles said, nodding sympathetically. "But you seem to handle it well."

"Thank you, Your Grace," Lady Catherine said,

her cheeks coloring slightly. “Still, I wish for it to end.”

“It will soon enough.” Charles smiled at her. "Once we announce our engagement, the gentlemen callers will turn their attentions to other ladies."

Lady Catherine lowered her gaze, her fingers playing with the lace on her parasol. "I certainly hope so. It is the main reason I agreed to this deception."

Her statement piqued his curiosity, and he asked, "What are the other reasons?"

Her blush deepened, and she looked away. “Nothing, truly. Forget I mentioned it.”

He made a mental note not to forget anything she mentioned—ever. But he would not press her now, for he had no desire to send her running. He needed her continued cooperation if he were to achieve his goal. Perhaps in time she would feel comfortable to divulge her secrets.

"As you wish," he said.

They lapsed into a comfortable silence, the only sounds coming from the rustling of the leaves and nearby birds. Lady Catherine shifted on the bench. "Your Grace, may I ask you a question?"

"Of course. You may ask me anything," Charles replied, turning to look at her.

She took a deep breath before speaking. "Why did you suggest this plan of a fake engagement? Surely, there must be other ways to achieve your goal?"

He smiled wryly. "There are always other ways, Lady Catherine. But none that would be as expedient or effective. As for my motivation, I no longer want to be hunted by marriage minded missis and their mamas. When I discovered you were also looking for a way to escape unwanted attention, it seemed the perfect solution for us both."

Lady Catherine furrowed her brow. "I understand the desire to escape from the marriage mart, Your Grace. But as a duke you have a duty to marry and continue your family line. Would it not be easier for you to take a wife and have done with it? Why damage your reputation further?"

Charles studied her for a moment before answering. "It is not so simple, Lady Catherine. I cannot marry any lady and move forward. I need a wife who can meet the expectations of the *ton*, one who can handle the demands of being a duchess and who I can trust to be a faithful and supportive partner. Whoever I marry will be the mother of the next Duke of Bedford. She cannot be whatever title hunting miss snags me, or whichever lady stumbles across my path first. Besides, I am not of a mind to give up my bachelorhood just yet. Not while I am still young."

"I see," she said, nodding in understanding. "You are lucky to be a man and have the opportunity to decide when you marry and how you live your life," Lady Catherine said, searching his face. "Women are not granted the same freedom."

"You will gain your freedom, Lady Catherine," he said, taking her hand in his. "If that is what you truly desire, I have no doubt you will achieve it."

She gave a weak smile, and the sight tugged at his heart. He rushed to reassure her, saying, "Truly, Lady Catherine. I will see to it."

She laughed. "Now you are being outrageous."

"Not at all," he said, giving her hand a squeeze. "I am most serious."

Just then a servant approached them, announcing the Duke of Thorne was looking for Lady Catherine and wished to speak with her privately. Charles stood and bowed, allowing her to take her leave.

As she walked away, Charles couldn't resist stealing one last glance at her. She was a complex woman, one who had secrets and motivations he couldn't quite grasp. But he was determined to understand her, to uncover all of her hidden depths. He could not say why, but she fascinated him.

He waited for a few moments before strolling back into the house, his mind already racing with plans for their next meeting. The game had only just begun, and he was eager to play it to the end. If he were honest he would admit he was eager to spend more time with her, too.

Tristin approached Charles as he entered the house, his eyes filled with disapproval. "Your Grace," he said, bowing stiffly. "I must speak with you at once."

Charles raised an eyebrow. "Is something the matter, Tristin?”

Of course he knew what Tristin was about. Knew Tristin would be the first to question his intentions where Lady Catherine was concerned.

Tristin glanced around the room, his attention moving over the other guests before returning to Charles. "It concerns my sister, Your Grace, and is best discussed in private."

Charles feigned ignorance, though in reality he had expected Tristin to confront him. His friend knew him all too well and Catherine was his sister, after all. Tristin had a duty to protect her. "Very well."

Tristin strode from the parlor, his stride long and footfalls heavy.

Charles followed, closing the door behind them when they entered the study. "Now, what is so pressing, Tristin?" he asked, his tone nonchalant.

Tristin glared at Charles. "What is your sudden interest in my sister?" he asked, his voice low, threatening.

"She is a beautiful woman and of marriageable age. I am courting her." Charles moved with confidence to the sideboard and retrieved a brandy decanter.

"You cannot expect me to believe you are suddenly of a mind to take a wife," Tristin said, indignation coating his every word. "Do not forget that I know you better than most. You are a rogue and as of a fortnight ago, had no plans to marry before exhausting your youth."

"Plans can change." Charles filled a tumbler with brandy, then took a sip. "I find your sister to be a rather intriguing lady and wish to know her better. Is that a crime?"

Tristin crossed his arms over his chest. "It is if your intentions are dishonorable."

"My intentions are anything but dishonorable," Charles replied, setting down his glass. "I have no desire to hurt your sister, Tristin." At least in that he was telling the truth. Charles meant to protect Lady Catherine regardless of how doing so might harm him. After all, he was a wealthy duke. His misdeeds would be forgiven, where as her indiscretions would not.

Tristin scowled. "Intentions be damned! You will hurt her, for we both know you have no intention of marrying her and even if you did, she won't have you."

Charles smirked. Tristin did, in fact, understand him well. Unfortunately, that meant Charles would have to trust his friend. He would have to tell Tristin the truth. God willing, Tristin would not force an end to his and Catherine's charade once he knew what they were about.

He took another sip of brandy, allowing the liquor to warm his throat as he glanced at his ring. "I am aware of that, Tristin. It is the very reason we have come to an arrangement. One that suits us both. And as a fellow wayward duke I am enlisting your help."

Tristin peered. "An arrangement? What kind of arrangement?"

Charles took another sip of brandy. "Lady Catherine is tired of being hounded about marriage and entertaining gentlemen callers, while I am tired of being hunted by women who only want my title and fortune. We have agreed to a fake engagement. Don't you see how perfect it is? The *ton* will believe we intend to marry and therefore everyone's match-making efforts will be directed elsewhere."

Tristin shook his head. "Catherine is my sister, and I will not have her getting hurt by your games. What do think will become of her once the truth is discovered? She will be ruined. Ostracized. Doors will be closed to her. I will not stand for it!"

Charles sighed. "I have no intention of hurting her. Besides, your sister is an intelligent woman, do give her some credit. She would not have agreed if we did not have a good plan for ending the engagement."

Tristin's stern expression softened slightly. "What kind of exit strategy have you devised?" he asked, his voice laced with suspicion.

Charles leaned back against the desk and drew a deep breath before answering. "We have agreed that when the time is right, I will have a public liaison after which Catherine will call off the engagement. No one will blame her for coming to her senses, and her reputation will remain intact."

Tristin looked unconvinced. "And what happens

to Catherine after that? What if you are wrong and she is cast out of good society?"

Charles could see the worry etched on Tristin's face. He knew his friend loved his sister deeply and would do anything to protect her. But Charles was equally determined to make this plan work.

"I will ensure Catherine is not ostracized," he said firmly. "I will use my influence to ensure she is still invited to all the important events, and that she has a place in society. Hell, I will defend her choice in jilting me. And if necessary, I will offer her my protection. Further, I will call on the other wayward duke's to open their doors to her. Society cannot scorn a lady who is welcomed by duke's and their heirs."

Tristin seemed to consider this for a moment before sighing heavily. "I see why the two of you wish to carry this out, but I still have my reservations."

"I understand," Charles said, standing up. "And I give you my word as both your friend and a gentleman, I will do everything in my power to protect your sister's reputation and ensure she is not hurt."

Tristin hesitated for a moment longer, then nodded. "Very well. I will agree to this... arrangement, but on one condition."

Charles nodded. “Name your condition?"

"I will chaperone every second you spend with Catherine. And I will have your word as a gentleman that if something goes wrong, you will marry her."

"That is two stipulations." Charles sat his tumbler on the sideboard.

"Do you agree?" Tristin said, his tone brooked no argument.

"You have my word." Charles grinned. "I plan to take her on a picnic tomorrow. Bring your own food."

“Indeed I will, and my pistol as well."

Charles chuckled as he placed his hand on Tristin's shoulder. "There will be no need for pistols."

Tristin shrugged off Charles's hand, his expression serious. "I am not joking, Your Grace. If anything improper happens between you and my sister, I will not hesitate to shot you."

Charles sobered. "I understand, Tristin. I will not cross any boundaries where Lady Catherine is concerned."

Tristin nodded, his gaze unwavering. "Good."

Charles nodded, the weight of their agreement settling heavily on his shoulders. He had never made such a pact with anyone before, especially not over something so serious. Bloody hell, he had promised to marry Lady Catherine if it became necessary to protect her. All the same, he was determined to see this through. He would protect Catherine while enjoying the season, and he would ensure their plan went off without a hitch.

Charles moved to the door before turning back to Tristin. "There will be no need," he said. "Now, if you will excuse me, I have matters to attend to."

Five

The sun shone brightly overhead, casting a golden glow on the verdant landscape. As they strolled together, Catherine's eyes lingered on the muscled contours of the duke's arm, exposed by his well-fitted jacket. She couldn't help but imagine what it would feel like to be held by him.

Nonsense.

She had to protect herself from foolish thoughts and longing. Their courtship was a pretense for their coming fake engagement. It was all a game designed by them to avoid marriage. This was not real and neither would she wish for it to be.

Catherine sighed, relishing the warmth on her

face as a gentle breeze rustled the leaves. "It is beautiful here."

He smiled down at her. "Indeed. Though I daresay not as beautiful as you, my lady."

A faint blush warmed Catherine's cheeks at his bold compliment. "You flatter me, Your Grace."

"We must keep up appearances," he said, giving her a roguish smile. The duke reached for her hand, his large one engulfing hers.

The heat of his touch permeated her glove to soak into her hand, and a jolt of awareness shot through her. "Then we shall have to continue flattering each other, won't we?"

His eyes gleamed with humor and something more heated that made her pulse race. In the time since they'd entered this arrangement, she'd developed an appreciation for Charles' noble brow, intense brown eyes, and the powerful line of his jaw. It should come as little wonder that she would react to the touch of such a handsome man. It meant nothing.

She opened her mouth to respond when a familiar voice called out, "There you two are!"

To her surprise, Tristen, emerged from behind the greenery, brushing dirt off his pristine black coat.

"Your Grace, Catherine," Tristen greeted them, his tone playful but his eyes sharp. "I hope you don't mind if I join you."

"Tristen!" Catherine exclaimed, annoyance lacing her words. With her brother so close she and Charles wouldn't be able to speak freely and would have to be extra careful to keep up their pretense of a genuine courtship. "What are you doing here?" She asked.

"Merely ensuring my sister's honor remains intact," he replied smoothly, a trace of a smile playing on his lips.

"I have a maid and two grooms along as chaperones. There is no reason for you to be along as well." She cast a worried glance toward the duke.

"On the contrary, dear sister." Tristan clapped the duke on the back, his expression lighting with mischief as he turned to the duke. "I cannot have my sister alone with a rake like you now, can I?"

"You wound me," the duke protested.

"Tristin," Catherine said, shooting him a quelling look. If she gave away their secret, all would be lost. "Shall we start the picnic, then?"

Tristan nodded and offered his arm to help her sit on the blanket the duke's footmen had laid out. Catherine settled in, all too aware of the duke seating himself close beside her, his arm brushing hers, sending sparks of desire through her.

"Tristen, I must say, your presence here has caught us by surprise," Catherine said, attempting to maintain her composure and wishing to be rid of him. Playing the devoted couple with servants who were out of earshot was one thing, but having her brother so near… It was an entirely different matter. Tristin was likely to see right through their pretense.

"Has it now?" Tristen mused, helping himself to a cucumber sandwich. "Dear sister, I have been quite curious about this sudden courtship of yours. And when I learned of your plans for today, I felt it necessary to ensure propriety was maintained." He glared at the duke. "Let us not forget that His Grace and I are old friends. I know him better than most and cannot in good conscious leave my baby sister alone with him."

"Tristen, this is hardly necessary," Catherine protested, her cheeks flushed with embarrassment. "We are simply enjoying a pleasant afternoon together."

"Ah, but you are courting, are you not?" Tristen asked, fixing them both with an unwavering gaze. "And as such, appearances must be maintained."

"Very well, Tristin," Lady Catherine conceded,

frustration evident in her voice. "But know your presence here is uninvited and unwelcome."

"Unwelcome, perhaps," Tristen replied, smirking as he bit into the sandwich. "Yet necessary, all the same."

Catherine exhaled a frustrated breath. "Tristin, really—"

"He knows," the duke said, peering at Tristen. "He has agreed to keep our secret and go along with our charade so long as we allow him to act as chaperone."

"Y-you know?" Lady Catherine stammered, her heart pounding in her chest. "How?"

"He was suspicious and confronted me, as he knew neither of us wished for marriage and knows us both too well to be deceived." The duke pulled two wineglasses from the picnic basket. "I thought it best to be honest with him. He will be a better ally than enemy."

"Indeed," Tristen confirmed, his tone grave. "And while I can appreciate the reasoning behind your charade, I cannot allow it to continue without proper supervision. As your brother, it is my duty to protect your honor and reputation."

"Tristen, I gave you my word as a gentleman that Lady Catherine's virtue is safe with me," the duke declared, his voice firm. He handed Catherine a glass of wine.

"Be that as it may," Tristen said dismissively, "I shall remain vigilant. Now, let us enjoy this lovely picnic, shall we?"

"Indeed." Catherine bit back her embarrassment and anger. She resigned herself to an afternoon of keeping up appearances for the servants' benefit while under the watchful eye of her brother. At least the apple tarts would be delicious. She only wished she could enjoy them, without her brother's interference.

Catherine picked at her tart, stealing glances at the duke when she dared. He seemed unbothered by Tristan's presence, casually discussing the latest parliamentary session and new shipping ventures over bites of ham and cheese.

Catherine envied his poise. Every word from Tristan's mouth made her stomach twist into knots, certain he would change his mind at any moment and ruin their plan.

As if sensing her discomfort, the duke reached over and took her hand. The warmth of his palm eased her anxiety. "Are you not enjoying your tart, darling?" His voice held a teasing lilt. "Cook will be quite put out if you don't finish it."

She forced a smile. "My apologies. I find myself quite distracted." She squeezed his hand in thanks, hoping he understood her meaning.

"Indeed," Tristan said, eyeing their joined hands. "Though I cannot fathom what has you so distracted. The Duke isn't all that handsome."

Charles barked out a laugh. "I beg to differ. Many a lady has swooned in my presence."

"And yet only one has captured your heart."

Catherine fought not to roll her eyes at the exaggerated sentiment.

"How lucky she must be," the duke said, mischief and good humor in his gaze.

Tristan made a disgusted noise, but Catherine noticed the twitch at the corner of his mouth. At least he seemed to enjoy their nonsense, even if she did not.

And why wasn't she? There was no reason for her to be cross or embarrassed. Tristin was her brother. He would do nothing to tarnish her reputation, so surely he would not reveal her and the duke's deception. Besides, the whole point of the charade was so that she and the duke could enjoy the season. She'd not allow Tristin to ruin everything.

"Indeed." The duke gazed at her. "I am the lucky one."

The warmth in his eyes stole her breath. For a moment, she could almost believe he'd meant it. Nonsense. She laughed, determined to enjoy herself. This was all for show, a game they were playing. And games were meant to be fun.

She would play her part well and enjoy every moment of the season. She glanced at her brother. Wether or not Tristin approved.

The duke gave her hand another squeeze, as if he sensed the tumult of her thoughts. The simple gesture was enough to steady her, and she offered him a small smile before turning her attention back to her tart.

After several moments of tense silence, Tristan set down his plate. "So, when is the happy day to be? Have you set a date for the wedding?"

Catherine blinked, surprised by the question. She and the duke had neglected to work out the finer details of their fictional betrothal.

The duke smoothly covered her hesitation. "We are still discussing the particulars. Sometime this fall, I should think. In order to get us through the hight of the season."

His gaze met Catherine's and she nodded.

"You will have to do better if you want people to believe this is a love match." Tristan said, one brow lifting in disbelief. "Forgive me, but you should have well-prepared answers to such questions if you want people to believe this farce. You are a duke and," he pinned Catherine with his grey eyes, "you are a duke's daughter. Everyone will be curious."

"Mind your own business. And keep your voice down lest the servants overhear," Catherine seethed.

"You are my business," Tristen said, his voice low.

The duke stretched out his long legs and leaned back on one elbow, the picture of nonchalance. "Catherine is the woman I intend to marry, and I see no reason to say much else."

"Besides," Catherine added, "We have not announced our betrothal yet. When we do, we can say we are content with a small, private ceremony to be held this fall."

"Precisely, right," the duke said. "We will keep the entire business simple."

"There is nothing simple about deceiving everyone you know." Tristan's gaze narrowed. "One misstep, and Catherine's reputation will be in taters."

Catherine's cheeks warmed, hating that he spoke the truth. She had spent years following the rules society laid out for young ladies. Still, she thought the risk to be worth the reward.

Even if their subterfuge was discovered, she

would get what she ultimately wished for—her freedom. A shiver of unease went through her. Unless she and the duke were forced to marry over the scandal of it all. She snuck a glance at him. Even then, would it be so bad to marry him?

The errant thought came unbidden, and she tensed. The duke was not the right man for her. He was simply a means to an end, a way out of this intolerable husband hunting business.

Nothing more.

And she would do well to remember it.

Six

In the days that followed, the Duke of Bedford became a constant presence in Catherine's life. His steadfast commitment to their plan served as a balm to her frayed nerves, easing the unease she felt after the picnic with Tristen. Each afternoon began with his arrival at the Thorne townhouse. He escorted her to teas, garden parties, balls, and musicals, all under the watchful gaze of her siblings and London's high society.

"Your grace," Lady Catherine greeted him one bright morning, as she descended the marble staircase to join him in the entrance hall. The sight of the duke in his impeccably tailored coat and breeches sent a shiver of excitement down her spine, an emotion she quickly tried to quell.

She knew she must keep up appearances, but the way his words and actions affected her made it increasingly difficult as the lines between reality and fiction blurred.

"Good day, my lady," the duke replied, bowing deeply before offering his arm. "I trust you slept well?"

"Indeed I did," she answered, allowing herself a small smile. As they exited the townhouse, she couldn't help but notice the curious glances from passersby—proof their courtship had become the talk of the *ton*.

"Are you prepared for the coming ball?" he asked in a hushed tone as they strolled through the bustling Mayfair streets en route to a nearby garden party.

"The ball," Lady Catherine echoed, her heart skipping a beat. "Yes, as ready as I can be." Her thoughts raced, trying to imagine how her family and high society would react to the announcement of their betrothal. In a few short days, they would set their plan into full motion.

"Trust me, Catherine," the duke whispered, leaning closer, his warm breath sending a thrill down her neck. "Everything will go perfectly."

As the days passed and the ball drew nearer, Lady

Catherine found herself torn between anticipation and dread. She couldn't shake the feeling that their ruse would be exposed. Her siblings' scrutiny weighed heavily on her—Tristin's knowing glances, Elizabeth's excitement over Catherine's courtship, and most of all, Olivia and William's pleasure in the fact she was allowing herself to be seriously courted. Their enthusiasm for her to marry sent a stab of regret through her heart. Everyone would be overset when she jilted the duke, and she detested the idea of causing them a moment's distress.

Still, she needed her freedom if she were going to continue her work at the orphanage. Those poor children needed her far more than she needed a husband. To think of all the good she could do as the duke's affianced, and even more so when she gained control of her dowery... How could she possibly change her mind and take a husband? She simply could not.

Not the duke, and certainly not another gentleman. Not that the duke wished for a wife. He certainly did not, she reminded herself. The fact she had to remind herself grated her nerves.

"Your Grace," Catherine said the next evening as they relaxed in the shadows of her family's garden during a musical soiree. "What if... what if we cannot convince everyone? What if they see through our deception?"

"They will have no reason to question our sincerity," he reassured her, his voice firm yet gentle. "Regardless, many marriages are agreed to for reasons other than love. We are more than capable of seeing this through, no matter the reception our announcement receives."

As the last notes of the music faded into the night, Catherine allowed herself to be enveloped in the duke's embrace, seeking solace in his strength and resolve.

Until Tristin cleared his throat, reminding them he was nearby and keeping his ever present gaze on them.

They moved apart as she prayed their plan would succeed. Prayed the announcement of their betrothal would be met with joy and celebration rather than suspicion and doubt.

And so, as the day of the ball arrived, she steeled herself for the task ahead, her heart aflutter with a mix of hope and trepidation. For better or worse, their lives were about to change, and all of London would bear witness. Her drawing room would empty of gentlemen callers—at least those seeking her company—and she would have peace.

The night of the ball arrived. The ballroom was aglow with candlelight that flickered across gilt mirrors and crystal chandeliers. Guests in silks and satins of every hue swirled across the gleaming parquet floor, spinning through the intricate steps of a country dance.

In the center of it all was Charles, his arm around Lady Catherine's waist as they moved together with practiced ease. Her hand was small and soft in his, her smile radiant as she gazed up at him through long lashes.

Desire coiled hot inside him, a blaze of longing fueled by the feel of her body pressed to his and the rosewater scent of her skin. It took all his restraint not to pull her closer, to lose himself in the depths of her sky-blue eyes.

He swallowed hard, forcing himself to remember this was all pretense. A charade to gain them a reprieve from the matchmaking efforts of the season. But with each passing moment, the lies grew harder to sustain.

Lady Catherine's chest rose and fell against his, her breath coming fast as the dance came to its climax. A flush stained her cheeks, her lips parted.

Charles could almost taste their softness, feel their yielding warmth under his mouth.

He could not deny his genuine attraction to her, nor could he deny the friendship that had blossomed between them.

The final chords of the music rang out, breaking the spell. After a moments hesitation, he released her, bowing as custom dictated. When he straightened, the longing reflected in her gaze nearly undid him.

She curtsied, a vision of loveliness that made his heart ache with longing. "Thank you, Your Grace. That was most...enjoyable."

Enjoyable. The word was woefully inadequate. But he merely offered his arm, guiding her off the floor as another tune began. "The pleasure was mine, Lady Catherine."

Though they had retreated to the sidelines, the warmth of her hand on his arm threatened to ignite him all over again. This temptation could not go on. It was against his nature to look temptation in the eye and not partake of it. He had to overcome her intoxicating presence before he did something unforgivable. Something that would drastically alter their plans.

He had to overcome the spark between them before he seduced her.

Or worse—fell hopelessly, irrevocably in love.

He had to announce the engagement and then he needed to put some distance between them.

Charles scanned the ballroom, searching for the Duke of Thorne. He finally spotted his quarry, speaking with several other gentlemen near the refreshment table.

His palms grew damp and he hesitated. What was he about to do? This mad, reckless plan had seemed so simple when he devised it. Now, faced with the actual moment, his courage nearly deserted him.

He glanced down at Lady Catherine on his arm, her eyes bright with merriment, her smile radiant. She leaned in closer, the scent of her—rosewater and woman—nearly undoing his frayed composure.

"Are you well, Your Grace? You seem distracted."

He swallowed hard. "Forgive me. I am about to approach your guardian and was considering how the conversation might end."

Her brows rose, but before she could speak, he began guiding her across the floor toward the Duke of Thorne. Each step increased his newfound anxiety, but he would not turn back now. Once this was done, he and Lady Catherine would have the true peace they were seeking. Both of them would be considered off the market. The two of them could enjoy the rest of the season without fear of being trapped and without the burden of unwanted attention.

As they approached, the Duke of Thorne glanced up, and for a moment Charles fancied he saw a flicker of wariness in the other man's gaze. But then Thorne's face smoothed into a polite smile. "Catherine. Your Grace. How do you fare this evening?"

"We are having a splendid time, thank you." Lady Catherine's gaze bounced between her brother and Charles, anxiety etched on her lovely features. "His Grace wishes to speak with you."

"Indeed." Charles smiled down at Lady Catherine before returning his attention to Thorne. "In private, if we may." He steeled himself, inclining his head to Thorne. Should the man refuse to grant his blessing, the plan would be in ruins.

And maybe that would be for the best.

Charles smoothed a hand over his jaw. Bloody hell, he had never doubted himself. He would not start now.

Thorne did not appear surprised as he nodded. "Certainly." He turned to his companions. "If you will excuse me, gentlemen."

The other men murmured their assent. Lady Catherine's hand tightened on Charles's arm, her unspoken encouragement hanging in the air between them. She released his arm and stepped back with a soft smile. "I shall await your return."

Charles watched her melt back into the crowd for a long moment before following Thorne to a nearby parlor.

His heart pounded as he faced Thorne, searching for the right words. He had never asked for a lady's hand in marriage and was not entirely comfortable doing so now. His palms grew sweaty as he faced her brother. Something about this moment felt all too real despite his and Lady Catherine's arrangement.

When the words came at last, they tumbled forth in a rush.

"Your Grace, I have come to ask for your sister's hand in marriage."

Thorne's expression shuttered, his gaze turning speculative. "I cannot say this is...unexpected. However, you have only been courting for a short time. I daresay a proposal at this juncture seems hasty."

Charles plunged ahead with the deception. "I care deeply for Lady Catherine. She is beautiful, intelligent, and kindhearted. I would be honored to make her my wife."

"Do you?" Thorne studied him for a long moment one brow arched. "Forgive me for being blunt, but you have shown no particular interest in Catherine before and you have met her dozens of times over the years. Why the sudden change of heart?"

Charles swallowed, scrambling for a suitable explanation. The truth was impossible, so he settled for a half truth instead. "I was not ready to settle down. I was a rogue, and she is a lady. Furthermore, she is Tristen's sister and, as you know, he is among my closest friends. I would not betray him by dishonoring his sister. But now, my being marriage-minded and seeing Lady Catherine in a new light..." He trailed off with what he hoped was a sheepish smile. "She would make me the perfect duchess."

Thorne did not appear convinced, but he nodded. "Very well. My sister's happiness is my primary concern. If she wishes to accept your suit, you have my blessing." His eyes hardened. "But know this—if you hurt her, if you break her heart or treat her unkindly, it will not be Tristin you have to worry about. I will make you regret the day you were born."

Charles inclined his head. "I understand, Your Grace. You have my word that I will do everything in my power to ensure Lady Catherine's happiness and well-being." The pledge rolled off his tongue with ease, for he meant every word. Despite the nature of his and Lady Catherine's relationship, he cared for her and would always look after her.

Another searching look, then Thorne sighed. "So be it. We shall announce the betrothal tonight." He offered his hand, and Charles shook it. The thrill of victory surged through him as he followed Thorne from the parlor.

Thorne strode into the center of the ballroom with his wife Olivia at his side. He lifted his hands and the lively strains of the orchestra trailed off, everyones attention turning to the Duke and Duchess of Thorne.

"My friends, I have an important announcement. My sister, Lady Catherine, has consented to marry the Duke of Bedford."

A stunned silence, then applause and cheers erupted around them. Lady Catherine blushed prettily as she curtsied to the applauding guests. Her gaze locked onto Charles's, a mix of emotions swirling in her eyes—triumph, fear, tenderness—he could not be sure, but it almost looked like joy.

His heart twisted. She knew this was a deception, knew he did not wish to marry her. Hell, she had made it clear she did not wish to marry him. Yet she smiled at him, a shy, tremulous smile that made him ache with guilt.

When the chance presented, Charles escorted Lady Catherine onto the balcony. The cool night air was a welcome respite from the stifling heat of the ballroom. His hand rested lightly on the small of her back, and he felt a spark of awareness at the contact. If she were any other woman... He pushed the thought away.

The balcony was deserted, the other guests still celebrating inside. A wrought-iron railing surrounded the balcony, intertwined vines and leaves silhouetted against the night sky, and the muted sounds of laughter and music filled the night.

Lady Catherine walked to the railing and gazed out at the garden below, silver moonlight glinting off the hedges. Charles joined her, standing perhaps a bit closer than propriety dictated. Her nearness stirred feelings he had no right to possess. And yet, he found himself in no hurry to escape her company. Not tonight.

He shouldn't be alone with her like this. Shouldn't be noticing the way the breeze teased strands of hair at her neck, or the graceful line of her throat as she swallowed.

"The gardens are lovely at night," she sighed.

Charles dragged his gaze away from the tempting sight of her pale skin. "Yes. Peaceful."

"I fear the peace will not last." She shot him a rueful smile. "We have managed to deceive my brother and Olivia, but what of everyone else? Society will be abuzz with the news of our betrothal, and everyone will be watching us."

"You're worried they will see through our ruse," he said.

"Aren't you?" She searched his face, eyes shadowed in the darkness. "This plan of yours is mad. I fear I am mad for going along with it. For enjoying..." She ran her tongue across her lower lip. "What if we cannot convince people we are truly in love? Tristin did not believe us and I daresay he will not be the only one."

"We shall have to be very convincing. Leastwise for a few weeks," he said, staring at her mouth.

She looked away with a shiver. "I suppose it is our only option."

Her hand rested on the railing, small and delicate in the moonlight. On impulse, Charles covered it with his own, the warmth of her skin seeping into his.

Her breath caught, and she turned to him with wide eyes. But she did not pull away.

His heart pounded as he gazed down at her. She was so close, her lips parted in surprise. It would be the simplest thing to bend his head and taste them.

He swallowed against the surge of longing. This was dangerous. He was playing with fire, and they would both be burned if he did not control himself. And yet...

He claimed her mouth in a searing kiss. His arms wrapped around her waist, holding her close as he ravished her mouth, indulging in the sweat taste of her—champaign and strawberries and woman.

She gasped, then rose on her toes, her hands tangling in his lapels.

This was dangerous, improper—he had to stop. Had to remember she was an innocent young lady. Had to control himself.

He pulled his lips from hers and took a step back, his hand capturing hers as she stared at him, breathless with kiss-swollen lips.

He had to remind himself yet again that no matter the attraction simmering between them, she did not care for him. She had agreed to this scheme for her own sake, not out of any tender feelings toward him. And neither of them wished to marry.

He forced himself to release her hand, the loss of contact causing a physical ache. "We should go back inside."

She nodded, color flooding her cheeks. "Yes. Before we are missed."

The space between them seemed charged with possibility and regret. Charles inhaled a shaky breath, trying to ignore the whisper in his mind, urging him to kiss her again.

He escorted her back inside, his hand burning where it rested on her back. As they entered the quartet played the first strings of the final waltz. Guests crowded the dance floor, spinning in time to the romantic music. He swept her onto the polished dance floor, holding her a bit too close as they danced.

When the waltz ended, Lady Catherine curtsied. "Thank you for a lovely evening, Your Grace." Her tone was polite but distant. "If you will excuse me, I believe it is time I rejoin my chaperones."

Panic flared in Charles's chest at her sudden coolness. He caught her hand before she could walk away. "Catherine, wait."

She paused but did not look at him. Her fingers were limp in his grasp.

Charles took a deep breath. "About what happened on the balcony... I apologize. My behavior was completely unacceptable. I should not have taken advantage in such a way."

She raised her gaze to his. "You are mistaken. You took no advantage." Her voice was cool. "We are betrothed, are we not? A kiss between us changes nothing." Her tone was nonchalant, but her blue eyes swam with a storm of emotions.

Charles frowned. "You cannot expect me to believe you when your eyes contradict your words."

"Believe what you will." Lady Catherine said flippantly as she freed her hand from his grip. "Good night, Your Grace."

This time he let her go, watching with a hollow feeling in his chest as she walked away.

Things had not gone at all as he planned. And he had a sinking suspicion this was only the beginning.

Seven

The sun dipped low in the sky, its golden light washing the path where Charles and Catherine strolled. Charles grasped Catherine's hand, As Tristin and Olivia trailed a discreet distance behind them.

A delicious shiver ran through her at his touch. Ever since their engagement announcement and the kiss that followed, she'd grown increasingly aware of his presence. The rumble of his laughter, the spice of his cologne, the warmth of his eyes when he looked at her.

Pretending to be in love with him came easy. Too easy, she feared. And now that they were under constant scrutiny, they had to play their roles at all times least someone discover the true nature of their relationship.

She glanced back at Olivia, then bit her lower lip. Her sister-in-law followed closely enough to hear their conversation. They would have to be careful not to give themselves away under her watchful eye. Even more so than normal, since she would likely report back to William.

A kiss would be rather convincing, and Tristin could not interrupt while Oliva was present. Not without betraying her and Charles, which he had promised not to do. Oh, how Catherine wished to kiss him, but dare she be so brazen?

"What are you thinking?" he asked.

She flushed. "Nothing of import."

He raised a brow. "You're a dreadful liar."

"And you're intolerably nosy." She smiled to soften the words, her mood lightening.

"Guilty as charged." He lifted her hand and pressed a kiss to her knuckles. "But I can't help wanting to know every thought in that beautiful head of yours."

"Can't you?" She laughed, a warm bubble of happiness welling in her chest. She would seize the opportunity. "Well, if you must know, I was thinking we've been engaged for nearly a fortnight, and you still haven't kissed me again."

He pulled her behind a hedgerow, one corner of his mouth hitching up. "Is that so?"

Her heart thumped. "Yes. I find it quite neglectful of you." She pouted, a mixture of playfulness and longing in her voice.

"Do you now?" He cupped her cheek, his palm rough and warm against her skin. "Then I sincerely apologize and aim to rectify my offense at once." He glanced toward the path.

Catherine swayed toward him, regaining his attention, and said, "See that you do."

His mouth claimed hers in a kiss that shattered her senses. She clung to his shoulders, drowning in the taste of him, the surrounding scents, golden light, and birdsong. He angled his head to deepen the kiss, his tongue tangling with hers for the briefest of moments before he pulled away.

She gazed up at him, breathless.

"Consider my offense rectified," he said, his voice low and sensual.

"Not quite." She wound her arms around his neck.

Charles let out a groan and kissed her again.

She floated through the rest of the day, her lips

still tingling from his kisses. She kept reliving those moments in the garden, the feel of his hands on her face, the taste of his mouth moving over hers. She knew she should not encourage his kisses and she most certainly should not crave them. But surely her reaction added a layer of reality to their ruse, which could only make their false love story more credible.

Still, she had to be careful, lest she forfeit her heart to the rogue. Perhaps less time together in the company of others, save for Tristin, would be wise. It would give them the opportunity to lower their guard and forgo the ruse for a short while.

Unfortunately, it was not to be for that evening at supper, Olivia announced preparations were underway for an engagement ball in Catherine and the duke's honor. "We shall invite everyone of note in London. It will be the event of the season!"

Catherine smiled along with the others, though inside she dreaded the ball. So many eyes would be upon her and the duke, judging and assessing. And she and Charles would be expected to perform like the happy, devoted couple they were pretending to be just when she had decided they needed more space.

And when had she started thinking of him as Charles rather than the duke?

She could not deny a fondness for him and smiled to herself deciding there was little harm in thinking of him in a less formal way. But kisses, those were dangerous indeed. There could be no more kissing.

After supper, Charles drew her aside. "Are you unwell? You've seemed distant all evening."

"I was thinking of the engagement ball," she admitted. "I don't relish being on display for all of London. I worry..." She shook her head. "Oh, forget I said anything. It does not signify."

He took her hand, his thumb stroking over her knuckles. "At least we shall endure the evening together. I much prefer your company to being chased by every debutant in London."

The warmth in his gaze made her pulse leap.

"Yes," she said. "Together."

The word was both a promise and a threat. She was no longer sure she would make it through their charade without falling deeply and irrevocably in love with her fake betrothed.

A sennight passed before William summoned Charles to his study. Catherine lingered outside the door, straining to overhear their conversation. Her heart pounded as William said, "The marriage contracts are ready. I would like them signed at once so we can announce your wedding date at the engagement ball this evening."

"Now?" Charles said, his voice tight. "So soon?"

"Is there a problem?" William asked. "You've had ample time to prepare. Unless..."

A heavy silence fell. Catherine's breath caught in her throat. Had Charles changed his mind? The time for that had passed. If he did not sign the marriage contract, she would be ruined. It was much too soon for her to beg off. She would look fickle if she jilted him this early after their announcement, no matter the circumstances.

"No, of course not," Charles said at last. "Just eager to get on with it, that's all."

Catherine released a shaky breath. The wedding was still on. Yet why did Charles sound so reluctant? Was it only for show, to make their charade more believable? Or did he truly wish to be free of his obligation to her? Was he too, worried about their growing attraction?

Some time passed before the study door opened, and Charles strode out. His face unreadable. "It's done," he said. "The contracts are signed. We're to be married this fall."

"Congratulations," Catherine said, forcing a smile. "We shall have to celebrate our good fortune."

"Yes, celebrate," he echoed, though his tone lacked any good humor. He bowed and took his leave, abandoning Catherine to wonder over his change of mood.

That evening, the ballroom was filled with light and laughter. White candles glowed in silver chandeliers, spilling over gowns of silk and satin, jewels and feathers. The string quartet played a lively dance as couples spun across the floor.

Catherine stood with her sisters, accepting congratulations from well-wishers. Louisa embraced her, blinking back tears of joy. "Oh, Catherine, I'm so happy for you! To think, this fall you'll be a bride," she said, her eyes sparkling. "I do hope the duke loves you as much as my Stephen loves me. Mark my words, you are certain to be happy so long as you love each other."

"Then I shall be happy indeed," Catherine said, forcing another smile though her heart ached. She did not like deceiving her family.

Louisa squeezed Catherine's hand. "I am quite certain you will be." She glanced across the space toward where her husband stood talking. "If you will excuse me, I find myself longing to join him now."

"Of course," Catherine said, releasing her sisters

hand. She watched with genuine happiness as Louisa made her way toward the earl.

Louisa had wed Lord Stone last season after the two of them were kidnapped and held for ransom. They seemed to be more in love each time Catherine seen them. Their devotion to one another was unmistakable, and it warmed Catherine's heart to see how happy Louisa and Stephen were. For an instant, she longed to find such happiness for herself.

A foolish and imposible notion.

She shoved the thoughts to the back of her mind as her cousin Othelia arrived wearing a lavender ballgown with lace and silver embroidery.

Catherine was shocked to see Othelia at the event. She had not attended any social gatherings for two years. And gone were her weeping veil and black crepe. With a wide smile on her face, she approached Othelia. "I am so glad you came."

"I thought this would be the perfect event for me to rejoin society," she said, hugging Catherine tight. "Regardless, I would never miss your engagement ball. Not even if I had to wear black and hide in corners." Catherine hugged her back, laughing at her cousin's outrageous words.

As the two women broke apart, Catherine's gaze

strayed to Charles. He was dancing with Juliet Fortescue, the Duchess of Cleburne. She was a vision in pale blue silk that matched her eyes. Charles leaned close, whispering in her ear, and Juliet laughed, the sound like tinkling bells.

A sharp pang shot through Catherine's chest at the sight. Why did seeing him with another woman in his arms bother her so? And Juliet of all women? It was ridiculous. Juliet and Olivia were the best of friends—so close that Juliet was like family. Even if Catherine's engagement was real, she'd have no cause for concern.

Catherine scolded herself. Stop being silly. This is all for show, remember? Part of the charade.

Even so, she could not ignore the hollow ache inside, or the bitter question that rose unbidden to her mind: What have I gotten myself into?

Othelia squeezed her hand. "Smile, Catherine. You're to be a duchess. You've landed the greatest match in all of England."

Catherine forced her lips into a curve, though her heart felt heavy as stone. "You're right," she said.

Othelia's gaze softened with sympathy. "It's only nerves. All brides have them. Do not fret, you and the duke will be very happy together. I know you will."

"I quite agree," Elizabeth said, playfully tapping her fan against Catherine's arm.

Catherine swallowed hard, willing her jealousy away, and wished with all her might she could stop her developing feelings for the duke.

As if he could feel her turmoil, Charles came to her side. He met her gaze, then held out a hand. "I should very much like to dance with my betrothed," he looked at Othelia and Elizabeth, "If you will excuse us."

"Of course," Othelia said, as she and Elizabeth nodded their approval.

Charles led Catherine onto the dance floor, pulling her into his embrace.

The ballroom was filled with light and laughter, the music of the orchestra reverberating through the air. She felt as if she were floating, buoyed by joy and champagne, and Charles's arm wrapped around her waist.

Things had progressed rapidly since their first meeting in the garden. Their engagement had been announced, the marriage contract signed, and now here they were dancing at their engagement ball. A part of her she dared not give voice to wished this were real.

Catherine glanced up at Charles, her heart skipping a beat at the warmth and tenderness in his gaze. He had been solicitous all evening, complimenting her at every turn and seeking opportunities to show his pretend affection. She found she didn't mind such attentiveness in the least.

"What is going through that pretty head of yours now?" he asked softly, lowering his mouth to whisper near her ear.

"Nothing." She sighed, leaning into his embrace. "Only how glad I am to have most of the engagement business over so we can start enjoying the season."

A wicked grin curved his mouth. "And here I thought we already were. I will make it my personal duty to ensure you enjoy every moment from here on."

"Promises, promises," she teased.

His arm tightened around her. "Promises I fully intend to keep."

The music swelled to a crescendo, the notes joyful and triumphant. Catherine smiled up at him, not sure whether she should be excited or afraid.

Eight

The sun shone through breaks in the clouds, its golden light caressing Catherine's cheeks as the phaeton rolled along the winding country lane. A light breeze rustled the leaves in the hedgerows and carried the earthy scent of loam and greenery.

Catherine breathed deeply, relishing the heady combination of sensations. Beside her, Charles's thigh pressed warm against hers, his arm brushing hers as he handled the reins. Her skin tingled where he touched her, heat pooling low in her belly.

She glanced at him from under her lashes, admiring the strong line of his jaw and the way the sunlight brought out the amber flecks in his brown eyes. He turned and caught her looking, a slow smile curving his lips.

"What are you thinking?" he asked, his voice a low rumble.

She shrugged, a flush staining her cheeks. "Just enjoying the ride."

"As am I." He reached over and took her hand, lacing their fingers together. "Your company makes any outing pleasurable, my lady."

The warmth of his hand seeped into hers, and she bit her lip against a sigh. They had started these drives and outings to create the appearance of a happy couple, a façade they needed to maintain. Now, she craved time alone with him for a far different reason. She enjoyed his conversation, his humor, the way he made her feel as though she were the most important person in the world when they were together.

Somewhere along the way, the pretense had given way to truth. Her regard for Charles had deepened into tender affection and a longing she didn't dare give voice to. She didn't know if he felt the same, if their closeness went beyond the requirements of their charade. She both feared and hoped he did.

Charles squeezed her hand. "I have come to enjoy the time I spend with you a great deal."

"As have I." Catherine smiled at him, hoping her eyes did not reveal the depth of her growing emotions.

Tristin rode up beside them on his horse.

"Really, you two. Must you behave so improperly?" Tristin frowned at them, though Catherine detected a glint of amusement in his eyes. "There is no reason to pretend affection when I am the only one about."

Charles grinned, utterly unrepentant. "It is best to stay in character least we grow too comfortable and make a mistake later."

"Hardly." Tristin snorted. "The two of you could rival Drury Lane's actors." He stared at his sister for a long heartbeat. "I know the truth, and yet, I am coming to believe there is more between you."

"Nonsense," Catherine scoffed. Heat flooded her face, even as Charles threw back his head and laughed.

Tristin sighed, shaking his head. "Honestly. Try to behave with some decorum, if you please." He peered at the duke. "And no more kissing. I'll not have my sister's reputation ruined. Do remember this is a charade. No marriage will take place."

"Fear not. We shall be models of propriety," Charles assured him. The wicked gleam in his gaze belied his words.

Catherine would wager Charles enjoyed irritating Tristin a great deal. It was no doubt why he continued to pretend affection when there was no need to do so. Regardless, she could not deny that she enjoyed his overtures. A fact she would surely come to regret.

With another exasperated sigh, Tristin urged his horse to keep pace with the phaeton. Clearly, he meant to prevent them from any displays of affection—pretend or otherwise.

Catherine bit back a smile, glancing at Charles from the corner of her eye. She could not help but find amusement in Tristin's behavior. He acted like an old mother hen guarding the henhouse. It was all too amusing, and more than a little heartwarming the way he protected her.

Charles shifted the reins in his hands and glanced at her. "Speaking of or engagement... Are you aware of the details of the marriage contract?"

Catherine's heart lurched at the serious tone of his voice.

"Such things are rarely shared with a lady." she said warily. "And as we do not intend to marry, I have put no thought into the terms. Is something wrong?"

"Nothing too onerous, I assure you." Charles gazed ahead, his thumb tracing circles over her knuckles. The sensation was strangely soothing and disconcerting all at once. "The usual allowances for pin money, servants, and a residence in town and country. An annuity of five thousand pounds per annum for you, should anything happen to me. All the usual things, except..."

"What?" Catherine turned, her gaze searching his face.

"Your brother had his solicitors add a clause requiring me to add two-thousand pounds to your dowery if I should fail to marry you for any reason."

She blinked at him, thinking she could not have heard him right. Only she had. "Your Grace, that is..." She shook her head. "Outrageous! Tell me you did not agree to such a term?"

"Of course I did. Thorne would have ended our arrangement at once if I had refused."

She stared at him, shock and anger surging through her. "That is a fortune. I cannot allow you to... I will not accept the money."

"Nonsense. You will need the funds if you are to live the rest of your life alone." His lips quirked.

"Besides, we have come this far and I am rather enjoying the respite from the matchmaking endeavors of the London season. It is a small price to pay to escape all the madness and know you will live the life you choose."

"It is too much." She shook her head. "I will not bankrupt you for the sake of this charade. I will tell William to burn the contract that I refuse to marry you on such terms."

"You forget, I am a duke and quite adept at managing my finances." His tone gentled. "Please, Catherine. Allow me to take care of you as I see fit. I would have it no other way."

She searched his face, struck anew by the earnestness in his gaze. He truly meant to provide for her, contract or not.

"Very well," she said at last. "On one condition—once I reach my majority, I will repay every pound."

"There is no need."

"There is every need." She lifted her chin. "I will not have your generosity taken advantage of, even if you do not mind."

He studied her for a long moment. Then a rueful smile curved his lips. "You are too stubborn by half, my lady. But I can see there will be no swaying you on this point."

"No, there will not."

"Very well. I accept your condition." He raised her hand to his lips, his gaze holding hers. "Now let us dwell on it no more."

"A-hum." Tristin cleared his throat.

Despite her brother's interference, pleasure swam within Catherine at the warmth radiating between her and Charles. She dared not contemplate his actions, however. This was but a game they played, one he did not yet wish to end, nothing more.

"As you wish," she said, her voice soft.

The phaeton rolled along at a leisurely pace, the sun dipping lower. Catherine relaxed into the seat, enjoying the warmth on her face and the pleasant company at her side.

Tristin rode alongside, having apparently forgiven them for their indiscretions. He regaled them with amusing stories and idle chatter, his mood lighthearted once more.

Catherine glanced over at Charles, finding him watching her with a curious expression. He gave her a smile and a small nod, as if coming to an unspoken decision.

A sudden thundering of hooves broke the intimate atmosphere, followed by the appearance of a rider racing toward them at breakneck speed. The man seemed wholly unconcerned with the potential danger he posed to others, his recklessness sparking a surge of fear within Catherine.

"Charles!" she cried, clutching his arm as the sound grew nearer.

"Steady now," he murmured, his calm demeanor doing nothing to soothing her nerves.

The approaching rider's proximity spooked the horses, causing them to rear up in fright. The phaeton jerked and swayed. Catherine turned to look toward Tristin. His horse reared and bucked.

Unable to maintain his balance, Tristin toppled from his saddle, his body hitting the ground with a sickening crunch.

"Tristin!" Catherine shouted as she stared helplessly at her brother.

Charles handed Catherine the reins as the reckless rider raced off. Her heart raced as he leapt from the phaeton and rushed to Tristin's side.

"Charles... My leg..." Tristin gasped, his face contorted in pain, sweat beading on his brow.

"Drink," Charles soothed, his voice thick with concern as he pressed a flask of whisky into Tristin's hand. He carefully assessed Tristin's injury, noting the unnatural angle of his leg. "It's broken. We need to get you back to the house."

"Do not move me," Tristin pleaded, his usual bravado replaced by vulnerability. "Do not leave me."

"I will not leave your side," Charles promised, His voice laced with concern. "Lady Catherine will go for help." He nodded at the flask in Tristin's hand. "Drink more. It will ease the pain."

Tristen nodded, then brought the flask to his lips for a long drink.

Charles hastily secured the frightened horses to a nearby tree, then turned to Catherine, who had climbed down from the phaeton and stood nearby.

Her heart pounded in fear as she glanced between Charles and Tristin.

"Can you ride to the house and fetch help?" Charles asked urgently, his words clipped.

"Yes," she replied without hesitation, her gaze on Tristin's pale face. She moved to his side and said, "Be strong, Tristin. You are going to be all right."

Tristin nodded, then squeezed her hand. "Go."

Catherine moved to her brother's horse, and Charles lifted her into the saddle. She took off at a gallop, determination thrumming through her as she rode for help.

~

The drawing room was in chaos when the doctor arrived.

Thorne paced by the fireplace, worry etched into the lines on his forehead. Tristin was laid out on the settee, his injured leg propped up on cushions, face pale and clenched in pain.

Charles kneeled beside his friend, grasping Tristin's hand. "The pain will pass, old man. I've sent for laudanum." His voice was tight with concern.

Tristin grunted. "Devil take your laudanum. I won't have my wits clouded when there are matters to attend."

The doctor cut away the bloodied pant leg, examining the swollen leg. "A clean break, but the bone has punctured the skin. This will need setting and stitches." He glanced at the men. "Hold him down, if you will."

Charles pinned Tristin's shoulders, murmuring apologies. Thorne took Tristin's hands in an iron grip. Tristin roared in agony as the doctor jerked the bone into place and began stitching the wound.

Sweat beaded Tristin's forehead. "Blast you all, let me up!" Through clenched teeth, he gasped, "Catherine..."

Charles leaned close. "Hush now. I will watch over Lady Catherine. You must rest."

"That is what I am afraid of. I need to..." Tristin sagged into the cushions, defeated.

"I have never failed you. Never betrayed you. I will not do so now," Charles said, his voice low so as not to be overheard. "Lady Catherine will be safe. You have my word."

The doctor finished his work and stood, washing his hands. "The leg must remain elevated and immobile for several weeks. No walking."

Tristin scowled. "Impossible. I have responsibilities—"

"Which will have to be delegated," the doctor said firmly. "If you wish to walk again, you must stay off that leg."

Tristin cursed under his breath, glowering at his traitorous limb.

Charles gave his shoulder a comforting squeeze. "All will be well. You are just going to have to trust me." He glanced toward the closed door, knowing Catherine was on the other side. "Trust your sister," he said, turning his attention back to Tristin.

Exasperated at the forced confinement, Tristin nodded his ascent. "It seems I have no choice."

Charles took his promise seriously. He would

ensure Catherine came to no harm. He would not ruin her, no matter how badly he wanted her. "Rest easy, old friend. I will treat her with the utmost respect."

"You had better." Tristin's eyes close as he spoke.

Charles patted his shoulder, then stood. No matter how difficult it became to resist the temptation she presented, he would have to safeguard Catherine's welfare—and her virtue. He owed it to Tristin and to their friendship.

Nine

Charles gave an easy smile as Catherine clutched his arm, the scent of roses and lush green grass heavy in the air. The garden party was alive with laughter and chatter, but all fell silent as they entered. He felt a surge of pride, knowing that everyone's attention was upon them.

"Ah, there they are!" exclaimed Louisa, Countess Stone, Catherine's vivacious older sister. "The soon-to-be-wedded couple! Come, come, tell us everything about the wedding plans!"

Catherine swallowed hard, casting a surreptitious glance at Charles.

The worry in her blue eyes tugged at his heart. They had not discussed the details of their never to occur wedding, leaving them unprepared for such interrogation.

"The… the wedding," Catherine stammered, her cheeks turning a becoming shade of pink. "It will take place this fall." She nibbled her lower lip. "We are still in the early stages of planning, aren't we, Charles?"

"Indeed," he replied smoothly, his warm hand giving hers a reassuring squeeze. "But we're certain it will be an affair to remember."

"Of course," added Catherine, her grip on his arm easing. "We want our special day to be simply perfect."

"Tell us about the gown, dear," coaxed Emma, the Viscountess of Linley, her violet eyes dancing with curiosity.

"Ah, the gown," repeated Catherine, grasping for inspiration. "I am considering a delicate ivory silk adorned with intricate lace and pearls. I believe it will be lovely."

"Sounds divine!" chimed Juliet, Duchess of Cleburne. "And what of the honeymoon? Any plans yet?"

"Actually," Charles interjected, seizing the opportunity to deflect attention away from themselves, "we'd love to hear about your own honeymoon experiences. I'm sure you all have wonderful stories to share."

"Ah, Paris!" sighed Louisa, grinning at the memory. "Stephen and I had the most marvelous time there."

Charles listened intently as Catherine's sister spoke of their romantic escapades. He could feel Catherine's hand tense where it rested on his arm, and he knew she was nervous. A moment of regret gripped him. It was his fault she was involved in this scheme.

"Lady Linley, how did you spend your honeymoon?" Charles asked.

Catherine gave him an admiring glance, her lips turning up in the slightest ghost of a smile.

"Venice," Lord Linley replied, a hint of a sparkle lighting his eyes. "A magical city, perfect for a newlywed couple."

"Indeed," Emma agreed, her voice wistful. "The canals, the gondolas... it's like stepping into another world."

Charles and Catherine exchanged looks of relief, having successfully shifted the guests' focus. But despite their outward composure, the tension between them was palpable. Charles couldn't help but wonder what lay ahead for their false engagement and what hell the remainder of the garden party might bring forth.

A sudden gust of wind rustled the leaves overhead, casting dappled sunlight across the guests as they mingled in the lavish garden. Catherine and Charles, still entwined, found themselves momentarily forgotten by their well-wishers. The scent of roses and lilacs filled the air, as laughter echoed through the lush foliage, while friends and family shared stories of their own romantic escapades.

"Your Grace," Charles began, addressing the Duchess of Cleburne with a roguish grin, "I heard you had quite the adventurous honeymoon in Greece."

"Indeed," replied Juliet, her lips curving in a mischievous grin. "We were nearly swept out to sea during a daring midnight swim!"

"Ah, yes," Giles, Duke of Cleburne, joined in, chuckling at the memory. "Nothing quite like a near-death experience to bring newlyweds closer together."

Catherine raised an eyebrow at Charles, her eyes alight with amusement. He couldn't help but return her smile, suddenly feeling lighter and more connected to her than he had ever imagined possible. He covered her hand with his, their fingers brushing suggestively.

"And what of you, Lady Othelia?" Charles asked.

"The Lake District," Othelia said, her tone lacking the wistfulness of their other companions. "The tranquility of the countryside suited us."

"Quite right," Catherine chimed in. She gazed up at Charles, and said, "Perhaps we'll brave a midnight swim of our own."

"Only if you promise not to let me drown," Charles quipped, his eyes dancing with mischief.

"Of course, darling," Catherine replied. "I'll always keep you afloat."

As the laughter continued around them, Charles found himself captivated by Catherine's intelligence and wit. The way her sapphire eyes sparkled when she laughed, or how her golden hair caught the sunlight, only served to make him question the line between their pretend courtship and his genuine attraction to her all the more.

"Charles, are you quite all right?" Catherine asked, concern etching her features as she noticed his sudden silence.

"Quite," he murmured, his voice barely audible above the merriment of the party. "I was just thinking about how fortunate I am to have found you, Catherine."

"Fortunate indeed," she replied softly, her gaze locked on his, their unspoken emotions simmering beneath the surface.

"Ahem," the Duke of Thorne cleared his throat, interrupting the charged moment. "Shall we continue the festivities? I believe there are games to be played."

"Of course, Your Grace," Charles said, tearing his gaze away from Catherine and offering a polite smile. Yet, as they turned to join the others, Charles couldn't help but feel a pang of protectiveness toward Catherine. As the lines between reality and their ruse blurred, it seemed inevitable that their hearts would become entangled in the game they were playing.

The very thought of hurting her nearly undid him at the very moment he realized it may already be a forgone conclusion. The way she looked at him—kissed him—laughed with him. It could not all be pretend.

Would she marry him if she fell in love? Or

would she stay steadfast in her determination to remain unwed? Did she already love him?

His chest tightened at the thought, and he had to wonder if his heart was already gone. What could he do if it was? He had promised her he would give her a way out. Promised her she would go on to have the life she desired. He blew out a slow breath and averted his gaze.

The sky had faded from blue to shades of pink, casting a warm golden light across the garden as laughter and conversation slowly faded into the background. Catherine leaned on Charles's arm, her relief palpable as they made their way toward the waiting carriage.

"I thought the questions would never cease," she murmured, her voice barely audible above the crunch of gravel beneath their feet. "Thank you for rescuing me."

"Always, darling," Charles replied with a half-smile, feeling the heat of her body pressed against him. As they climbed into the carriage, the door shutting behind them, Charles found himself suddenly aware of the intimacy of their surroundings. The small, dimly lit space was filled with the scent of Catherine's perfume, and he could hear the faint rustle of her skirts as she shifted beside him.

Bloody hell, he wanted her.

All of her.

Every smile, heated glance, and tender touch. Her kisses... He wanted to wake up beside her. To spend all of his days with her at his side. He wanted to argue with her, play with her, spend a life with her.

"Is something amiss?" Catherine asked, concern lacing her words. "You've been rather quiet since we left the party."

Charles hesitated, his eyes drawn to the gentle curve of her neck where her pulse fluttered just beneath the skin. He wanted to touch her, to feel the warmth of her body against his, but he couldn't shake the guilt that gnawed at him. Their engagement was nothing more than a farce, yet he found himself wishing it were real with every beat of his heart.

"There is no need to fret," he said finally, forcing a smile onto his lips. "I suppose I am merely tired from the day's events."

"It has been quite an exhausting day," Catherine agreed, averting her attention out the window to the rapidly darkening sky. "But we managed it well, don't you think?"

"Exceptionally so," Charles replied, his heart

swelling with pride and affection for the woman beside him. "I never imagined I would enjoy our charade so much."

"Nor did I," Catherine admitted, a soft laugh escaping her lips. "And I daresay we make a rather convincing couple."

"Indeed," Charles echoed, his voice strained as he fought against the urge to reach for her. He could really use Tristin's meddling right now. The thought put a temporary damper on his longing.

The silence that followed was heavy with unspoken words and emotions, the tension between them growing heavier with every passing moment. Charles could feel the weight of Catherine's gaze on him, and he knew she was waiting for him to say something, anything, to break the stifling quiet.

"Charles," she began hesitantly, her fingers fidgeting with a fold of her skirt. "Can I ask you something?"

"Of course," he replied, steeling himself for whatever question she might pose.

"Do you ever... do you ever wonder what it would be like if our engagement were real?" She asked, her voice barely more than a whisper.

The question hung in the air between them, and

Charles felt a shiver run down his spine. He wanted to tell her the truth, to confess that he had been pondering it, but fear held him back. How could he admit to such feelings when he knew she did not wish to marry?

"Sometimes," he finally conceded, his voice tight with emotion. "But we both know the reality of our situation. Right?"

"Indeed," Catherine agreed softly, though the sadness in her eyes belied her words.

As the carriage rumbled onward through the darkening streets of London, Charles couldn't help but feel as though they were leaving behind more than just the garden party. In the small, dimly lit space, with the scent of her perfume enveloping him and the heat of her body mere inches away, he realized he wanted Catherine more than he ever thought possible.

But the truth of their fake engagement loomed between them, a stark and unyielding reminder of the lie they had spun. And as they drew closer to her house, Charles couldn't help but wonder what the future held for them both.

He studied her. The dim glow of the carriage lantern cast flickering shadows across her face, highlighting the delicate curve of her cheek and the gentle parting of her lips. Charles could no longer resist the magnetic pull between them. Before either of them could think better of it, he leaned in and pressed his mouth against hers.

The kiss was a revelation—tender and passionate, underscored by the urgency of their unspoken desires. Their lips moved together in a dance as old as time, fueled by the intoxicating blend of vulnerability, trust, and attraction that had been building between them. Even as he warned himself of the potential consequences, Charles couldn't help but surrender to the overwhelming emotions coursing through him.

Catherine's fingers threaded through his hair, drawing him closer. The intensity of their connection deepened, and the world outside the carriage ceased to exist as they clung to one another, the lines between reality and fantasy blurring until all that remained was the raw, undeniable truth of their feelings for each other.

"Charles," Catherine whispered against his lips, her breath warm and sweet. "This... this is more than just our pretend engagement, is it not?"

Her words struck him, laden with the weight of both hope and fear. Charles pulled back slightly, the enormity of the situation settling over him like a cloak. He searched her eyes, seeking some measure of reassurance, and found only the same mixture of apprehension and longing that mirrored his own.

"Perhaps," he admitted, his voice barely audible above the rumble of the carriage wheels. "But what does it mean for us, Catherine?"

Catherine's gaze held his, unwavering in its intensity. "I do not know. Regardless, it is best if we go back to the way things were before. It is best to forget this."

He wanted to tell her they could return to their charade and continue on as if nothing had changed. But even as he thought it, Charles knew it was a lie—one he could no longer bear to tell. Something had changed between them, irrevocably altering the course of their lives. It was no longer a game for him, and he did not believe it to be a game for her either. But what did that mean? Where did it leave them?

"Perhaps not," he conceded, a mixture of fear and exhilaration coursing through him.

"We must forget," she murmured, her eyes shining with a fierce determination. "Fanciful thoughts will only complicate things. We must stick to our plan."

His chest squeezed at the determination in her

voice. Swallowing his objections, he said, "Then let us continue on the course we have set," Charles said, his heart swelling with equal parts love and trepidation. "And may the fates be kind to us as we navigate the uncertain waters of our future."

Ten

The following evening, Charles stood at the edge of the Chatsworth ballroom, his gaze fixed on Catherine as she moved gracefully among the dancers. He couldn't help but admire her poise and beauty, a delicate rose in a sea of opulence. Her golden curls were swept up in an elegant chignon, and her sapphire eyes sparkled with life.

He could not say precisely when the charade had become a reality for him, but he was determined to have her for his wife. He need only discover the reason she clung so hard to her freedom. Once he knew, he could overcome the obstacle and she would become his, for he had no doubt she shared his feelings.

"May I have this dance?" Charles asked as he approached her, extending a gloved hand. Catherine hesitated for a moment before nodding and placing her hand in his, allowing him to lead her onto the dance floor.

As they waltzed together, Charles felt the familiar warmth of desire stirring within him. But it was more than physical attraction that drew him to Catherine; there was something about her spirit, her independence, that intrigued him deeply.

"Forgive my impertinence," he began, "but I am curious as to why you have remained unmarried. A woman of your beauty and intellect has surely had many suitors, and yet you choose to remain unwed."

Catherine's cheeks flushed at his words, but her gaze remained steady and confident. "Marriage is not all it is made out to be, Your Grace. I have seen too many women lose themselves in the bonds of matrimony, and I would rather maintain my freedom."

"Your dedication to independence is admirable," Charles replied, genuinely impressed by her conviction. "But what occupies your time, if not the pursuit of a husband? You once told me you had several reasons for agreeing to our fake engagement. You can trust me enough to share them."

She stared deep into his eyes for long heartbeats, then said, "Promise me you will keep my secrets," her voice barely above a whisper, as if sharing a sacred confidence.

Charles nodded without hesitation, driven by his desire to understand her better.

"I spend time at an orphanage, teaching the girls to read, write, and conduct themselves like ladies. I provide them with an education they might not otherwise receive, in addition to lending my financial support when I am able."

"An orphanage?" Charles repeated, surprised by her admission. "You truly are a remarkable woman, Lady Catherine. I would be honored to see your work, if you would allow it. Perhaps I can lend my assistance as well."

Catherine looked at him skeptically, no doubt weighing the potential risks of his involvement. But Charles could see the fierce protectiveness come over her, and he knew she would do anything for those children.

"Very well," she said finally, "but only if you promise never to speak of this to anyone. Not even my family. The orphans need me and my brother the duke, has forbidden me to continue my visits. If he discovered the truth that I am still teaching them..."

"Of course," Charles agreed readily, touched by her devotion to the children. "I swear on my honor I will keep your secret."

"Very well. We will call at the orphanage tomorrow afternoon when we take our customary drive."

He pulled her closer, and she relaxed into his hold.

Charles couldn't help but feel as though he had unlocked a hidden part of Catherine's soul, and the closeness between them seemed to intensify with every step they took together. He was determined to remain by her side, driven by an undeniable attraction that went far beyond mere physical desire.

And so, as the music swelled around them and the dancers twirled in a sea of silks and satins, Charles knew they stood at the precipice of something new and thrilling—a connection that would change both of their lives forever.

God willing, it would be for the better.

The following morning, Charles waited for Catherine in his carriage, his anticipation building with each passing moment. He glanced out the window, his gaze trailing along the cobblestone streets of Mayfair.

Finally, Catherine appeared, her dark hair neatly

pinned beneath a simple bonnet, her eyes downcast as she approached the carriage.

"Good morning, darling," Charles greeted her warmly as he offered his hand to help her into the carriage.

"Good morning, Your Grace," she replied, accepting his assistance, her touch sending a thrill through him. As the carriage started moving, Charles noticed Catherine staring out of the window with a reserved disposition.

"Are you well, Lady Catherine?" he asked, concerned by her reticence.

"Quite well, thank you," she replied softly, her gaze meeting his for a moment before returning to the passing scenery. Charles found himself entranced by the vulnerability he sensed beneath her guarded exterior and felt an irresistible urge to protect her.

"Do, tell me more about your work at the orphanage?" Charles ventured, hoping to encourage conversation.

"Of course," Catherine answered, a hint of warmth entering her voice. "I visit twice a week, Mondays and Thursdays, while William believes me to be at tea with old finishing school friends. The children are smart and eager to learn. I leave them with instructions for practice and further studying. They take it very seriously. All of the older girls can read and write and they help teach the younger girls while I am away. It brings me great joy to see them learn and grow."

Charles was struck by the passion that ignited within her as she spoke of the orphans. He found himself increasingly drawn to this remarkable woman who dedicated herself so selflessly to others. A powerful urge to lend his own assistance gripped him along with a niggling question. "Is your work at the orphanage the reason you do not wish to marry?"

Her eyes shuttered as she averted her gaze.

It was all the answer Charles required.

Upon their arrival at the orphanage, they were greeted by a chorus of excited voices as the children clamored around Catherine, their adoration evident in their wide, hopeful eyes. Charles observed from a distance as she knelt to embrace a small girl with tangled hair and a shy smile.

"Good morning, Emily," Catherine said tenderly, smoothing back the girl's unruly locks. "Are you ready for your lesson today?"

"I-it is Wednesday, my lady," the girl stammered, her round eyes shining with admiration.

"You are quite right," Catherine said, giving the girl a hug. "What do you say to a Friday lesson?"

"Y-yes," the girl stammered, a smile spreading across her face.

As Catherine led Emily and the other orphans into a modest classroom, Charles marveled at the transformation that had taken place within her. The reserved woman he had shared the carriage with seemed to have vanished entirely, replaced by a vibrant, passionate force that captivated him completely.

"Today, we shall continue our practice of sewing," Catherine announced, distributing small pieces of fabric and needles to each child. As they began their work, she moved from one to the next, offering gentle guidance and encouragement.

"Remember, steady hands make for even stitches," she reminded Emily.

The small girl nodded vigorously, her tiny fingers deftly weaving the needle through the material.

Charles watched in awe as she nurtured and inspired the children, a fierce protectiveness swelling within him. He longed to be a part of her world, to support her in any way he could, yet he knew he must respect her wishes and maintain his distance.

"Your Grace?" Catherine's voice broke through his thoughts, and he realized she was standing before him, a questioning look in her gaze.

"Forgive me," he murmured. "I was simply... admiring your dedication to these children."

"Thank you," she replied softly, a hint of a smile touching her lips. "It is my greatest pleasure to help them."

"Your passion is truly inspiring," Charles said, his heart pounding in his chest as he met her gaze. "You are an extraordinary woman, Lady Catherine Breckenridge."

As their eyes locked, Charles felt the world around them fade away, leaving only the two of them and the undeniable attraction that crackled between them. With a quiet sigh, he tore his gaze away, focusing instead on the orphans who deserved all of her attention.

The next hour was spent touring the orphanage with the head mistress and Catherine. After being introduced to the boys, who occupied a separate wing and helping to serve the children dinner, Catherine led him into the yard. The sun had started its descent, sinking lower in the sky to cast a warm glow over the orphanage, and the faces of the children Charles had come to care for. Their laughter rang out, filling the air with a sound that was both heartwarming and heartbreaking. He couldn't help but think of all they had been through—and yet, here they were, still capable of finding joy amid their struggles.

He had never given any thought to orphans before. Hell, he never thought much about anything that did not directly affect him. Bloody hell, he had been a selfish bastard. Now his chest ached for the lost innocence—the forgotten and abandoned children. He would do more than lend financial help. He would bring a bill to parliament.

"Your Grace," Catherine said, her voice pulling him from his thoughts. "Would you like to join us in a game of tag?"

"Doing so would bring me great pleasure, my lady," he responded, his eyes gleaming with excitement. As he approached the group of eager orphans, a plan took shape in his mind. He knew he wanted to contribute to their happiness, to make a difference in their lives—and he would start by making a generous donation to the orphanage, but he would not stop there. He would draft a bill and see that Catherine had whatever support she needed to continue her work as well.

As Charles chased after the laughing children,

their wide smiles infectious, he found himself swept up in the simple pleasure of the moment. Unburdened by the weight of society's expectations, he felt an unexpected sense of freedom and connection to these young souls.

"Your Grace, you're it!" cried little Emily, her expression alight with mischief as she tapped his thigh before darting away.

"Very well, my dear," he replied, feigning indignation as he set off in pursuit, his heart swelling with affection for the children who scampered about the yard.

Throughout the game, Charles couldn't help but steal glances at Catherine, admiring the way her face lit up with each peal of laughter from the orphans. The sight stirred something deep within him, a yearning to be more than a distant admirer. With every interaction between Catherine and the children, his desire to support her work intensified.

When the game finally came to an end, with flushed faces and breathless laughter filling the air, Charles made his way to Catherine's side. Her joyous expression warmed him, and he found himself momentarily lost in her eyes.

"Lady Catherine," he began, his voice low and sincere, "your dedication to these children is nothing short of remarkable. I find myself moved beyond words."

"Thank you," she replied, a soft blush coloring her cheeks. "But it is they who inspire me."

"Regardless, I wish to contribute to their happiness—and yours. Therefore, I would like to make a significant donation to the orphanage." He held her gaze, his heart pounding.

"How incredibly generous of you," Catherine said, her eyes sparkling in the late afternoon sun. "I cannot express how much your support means to these children and to me."

"Your happiness and their well-being are of the utmost importance," he assured her, his resolve unwavering. "I am happy to provide my aid."

As they stood together amidst the fading light, Charles knew he had taken a step toward something greater than he'd ever known. With each passing moment, his affection for both the orphans and the woman beside him grew deeper, binding them together in a bond that transcended mere obligation or pretense. He would do anything to help the children and ensure Catherine's happiness. He was in love with her.

His days of being a rogue were behind him. And in that moment, he had but one regret—their fake engagement—and he would do all in his power to correct it.

The children lined up and waved farewell as Charles and Catherine climbed into the waiting carriage. As the carriage moved forward, Charles couldn't help but steal glances at Catherine. She gazed out the window, lost in thought, and her golden hair framed her face in soft tendrils.

"Are you well, Catherine?" he asked, his voice barely above a whisper.

"Quite well," she replied, turning to meet his gaze with a small smile. "I am simply... overwhelmed by your generosity."

Charles's heart fluttered at her words, but he struggled to quell the desire that stirred within him. He longed to reach out and touch her, to feel the warmth of her skin against his own, but he knew such actions would be improper. Instead, he focused on the steady rhythm of the carriage wheels and the faint sound of hooves against cobblestones.

"You make me want to be a better man," he said, allowing himself a brief moment to admire her. "I only wish there was more I could do."

"Your donation will make a substantial difference," she assured him.

Charles swallowed hard, his conflicting emotions

threatening to overwhelm him. He wanted nothing more than to take her in his arms and kiss her senseless, but did not want her to feel obligated to kiss him back because of his donation. And so they sat in silence, each lost in their own thoughts as the scenery outside the window blurred together in a symphony of colors.

"Lady Catherine," he murmured, unable to restrain himself any longer.

"Yes?" she asked, her gaze full of warmth.

He reached for her, their lips meeting in a tender, passionate union that seemed to bridge the chasm between them. Charles lost himself in the taste of her, his hands coming up to cradle her face as their kiss deepened.

She responded with equal fervor. Her fingers tangling in his hair as they clung to each other, desperate for each others touch.

He pulled his mouth from hers as the carriage jolted to a stop in her drive.

"Tomorrow," Catherine whispered, her voice trembling with emotion.

"Tomorrow," he echoed, his own voice thick with longing.

Eleven

Catherine strolled into the bright sitting room, eager to have tea with Othelia, though she wished she was not deceiving her. Still, the fewer people who knew the truth of her engagement, the better. She spotted her cousin, already seated at the delicate table adorned with a teapot and fine china cups.

"Othelia!" Catherine exclaimed, her voice lilting with genuine warmth. The two of them had been the closest of friends for most of their lives and had spent little time together these past several years due to Othelia's marriage, then quickly following mourning period. Catherine was ever so happy to have this time with her now. She strode effortlessly across the room, an easy smile on her lips.

"Ah, Catherine," Othelia greeted her with a fond smile. "I've been eagerly awaiting our afternoon respite and the chance to speak privately. It has been too long."

"Indeed," Lady Catherine agreed, settling into her seat. She reached for the teapot, the intricate floral pattern on the porcelain catching the sunlight.

As they poured the fragrant tea into their cups, steam rising like whispered confessions, the two women exchanged knowing smiles. They both understood the importance of these stolen moments away from the prying eyes of London society and their family.

"I have been out of society for so long. Tell me, what news have you heard of the latest scandal?" Othelia inquired, eager for the juicy details. "I am positively starved for gossip."

"Ah, yes," Catherine replied, her eyes sparkling with delight. "Lady Patience, Viscountess Green, was seen sharing a rather intimate dance with a certain dashing gentleman who is most certainly not her husband." She took a sip of her tea, allowing the sweet liquid to linger on her tongue. "Many believe they are having an affair."

"Good heavens!" Othelia gasped, raising a hand to her bosom in mock horror. "I've always thought

Patience to be a bit of a risk taker, but surely she would not be so reckless?"

"Perhaps it is merely an innocent flirtation," Catherine mused, her thoughts drifting to her own secret dalliances with Charles. How she longed to confide in Othelia the true nature of their engagement. She knew she could trust her cousin with such a delicate matter, but still...

"I fear I would not be a good judge," Othelia said. "It has been quite some time since I was out in society. Longer since I engaged in flirtation of any kind."

"Indeed," Catherine agreed. "You have mourned far longer than required. I am glad to see you engaging with life again."

"True enough," Othelia conceded, sipping her tea with a thoughtful expression. "It is only that I was so young when I married. All I know is being a wife and dutiful daughter. I am not at all sure what to do as a widow, but I am trying to acclimate."

"Might you remarry?" Catherine sipped her tea.

"I do not think so." Othelia delicately placed her teacup on the saucer, her hazel eyes meeting Catherine's with a hint of curiosity. "Catherine, dear, you know I care for you as more than a cousin. You are my best friend. We have shared so many secrets and dreams over the years. I am grateful for you and for our bond." She reached across the table and squeezed Catherine's hand.

"As am I," Catherine said, her throat tightening as her conscious ridiculed her for deceiving Othelia even as they spoke of friendship and shared secrets.

"Something seems amiss." Othelia gave a slight smile. "Are you experiencing bridal nerves?"

Catherine shook her head. "No, everything is perfect."

"Very well, then tell me, how are the wedding plans progressing?" Othelia brought a tea cake to her mouth and took a bite.

Catherine hesitated, toying with the lace edge of her own teacup. She could not continue lying to Othelia. Her heart pounded in her chest, but she knew she could trust her cousin. Drawing a deep breath, she met Othelia's gaze. "There is something I must confess. The engagement... it is not what it seems."

"Whatever do you mean?" Othelia asked, concern etched upon her face.

"The truth is," Catherine whispered, her voice barely audible above the clink of porcelain and rustle of silk, "our engagement is naught but a sham. A charade. We plan for me to cry off at the end of the season."

Othelia's eyes widened, and she leaned in closer, lowering her voice to match Catherine's confidential tone. "But why? You two seem so well-suited, and I know William and Olivia are thrilled with the prospect of the union."

"Indeed, they are," Catherine admitted, her fingers twisting the delicate lace nervously. "But this arrangement was never meant to be permanent. It was merely a means to an end—a way to appease my brother and maintain appearances while allowing the Duke of Bedford and I time to enjoy the season." Her eyelids closed for a heartbeat. "Neither myself nor the duke wish to marry anyone. Leastwise not at this time."

"Such a scheme is not at all like you. It must have been the duke's idea." Othelia sighed, her brow creasing with concern. "You must know these sorts of deceptions can have serious consequences."

"I am aware and thought the risk to be worth taking, for I did not wish to marry. Ever. But now," Catherine replied, her voice strained with emotion, "my heart was not meant to be part of the farce, but it seems fate had other plans."

"Are you saying you have developed feelings for the duke?" Othelia asked, her gaze searching Catherine's face.

"I have," Catherine whispered, her cheeks flushing with a mixture of embarrassment and longing. "And I fear my actions may have placed my heart in grave peril. The worst part of all is that he has no wish to marry. Leastwise, not this season, and he believes I never wish to marry at all."

"But you do want to marry him?" Othelia asked, concern radiating from her.

"No... Yes." Catherine shook her head. "I am not sure. I can imagine myself as his wife, but not with the freedoms I desire. I fear I would have to give-up a part of myself to become his wife and am not sure I am willing to do so." She waved a dismissive hand. "It matters not as he has no intentions of marring me."

"How can you truly know? You must tell him the truth, Catherine," Othelia urged, her voice firm yet gentle. "You owe it to yourself and to the duke to be honest about your feelings. I have seen the way he looks at you. Touches you. I believe he has a genuine interest in you."

"Perhaps you are right," Catherine conceded, a tear pooling at the corner of her eye. "But what if he does not love me?"

"There is but one way to find out, dear," Othelia

whispered, reaching out to squeeze Catherine's hand in reassurance. "You must speak with him."

"What if he returns my feelings but cannot support my dreams? What if he wished to keep me in a gilded cage? It is the very reason I had no wish to marry. I cannot allow a man to dictate my life."

Othelia's hazel eyes widened with concern as she took in Catherine's confession. "I understand your reservations and would never suggest you forfeit your own dreams. But you are falling in love," Othelia observed, a touch of sadness in her voice as she realized the depth of Catherine's dilemma.

"Against all reason and expectation," Catherine replied, her cheeks flushing with the heat of her confession. "It is both exhilarating and terrifying, for I know not what to do or how to proceed."

"Love is rarely simple, dear cousin," Othelia said with a sigh, her own experiences with love and marriage casting a shadow over her features. "But I believe honesty is the best way forward. The duke deserves to know the truth, as do you—for only then can you both decide what path your hearts will take."

"Thank you," Catherine whispered gratefully, her eyes shining with unshed tears. "It was never meant to be this way."

"Sometimes we have to trust in fate and in our

own intuition." Othelia reached for her teacup. "Trust yourself. You are a smart and capable woman. Everything will work out as it should, as long as you follow your own intuition."

Catherine forced a smile. "I daresay. I hope you are right."

Othelia reached out and placed her hand over Catherine's, offering a warm, supportive touch. "Fret no more, for I know I am."

"I shall not," Catherine said, then quickly added, "You must not breath a word of this to anyone. The last thing I want is a forced marriage."

"Your confidences are safe with me," Othelia assured, her tone full of empathy. "I know all too well the pain of a loveless marriage."

Catherine's gaze snapped back to her cousin, her curiosity piqued at this sudden revelation. She had always known Othelia's marriage to the much older Earl of Brighton had been arranged to save her family from financial ruin, but she had never heard her speak so candidly about her own feelings.

In fact, she had spent so little time with Othelia since her marriage that she scarcely knew a thing about Othelia and Lord Brighton's relationship.

"Othelia..." she began hesitantly, unsure of what

to say. But her cousin waved away her concern with a sad smile.

"Please, there is no need for sympathy," Othelia insisted, her fingers absently tracing the delicate rose pattern on the teacup before her. "My husband was kind enough, but our union was devoid of passion and affection. I often felt as though I were little more than an elegant ornament, placed upon his arm."

As she spoke, Catherine could see the weight of those memories pressing down upon Othelia's slender shoulders. The shadows of loneliness and longing lingered in her eyes.

"Love, true love, is a rare and precious thing," Othelia continued softly, her voice barely audible above the patter of rain against the windowpanes. "If you have found it with the duke, then I would not begrudge you the chance to explore what love has to offer—even if your engagement is a fabrication."

Her words resonated within Catherine, filling her heart with both hope and trepidation. Could she truly allow herself to follow her desires, even if it meant risking scandal and her family's disapproval?

"Thank you, Othelia," she whispered, her voice thick with emotion. "Your understanding means more to me than you can know."

"Then let us make a pact," Othelia suggested, determination etched across her features. "I swear on my honor as a lady of the realm I shall never reveal your secret to another soul. In return, you must promise me you will pursue your happiness, regardless of the obstacles you may face."

Catherine hesitated for a moment. "You must also swear to reclaim your life and find your own happiness."

Othelia grinned. "I vow I will."

Catherine nodded resolutely. "Very well. It is done."

"Excellent," Othelia smiled, raising her teacup in a toast. "To love, life, and all its complexities."

"To love, life, and all its complexities" Catherine echoed, clinking her own cup against her cousins before taking a long sip of the fragrant brew. As the warmth of the tea filled her, she felt a spark of courage ignite within her heart—a courage that would be needed if she were to navigate the treacherous waters of society and the perils of her own desires.

Twelve

Catherine rode beside Charles along Rotten Row nodding to their piers, her mare keeping perfect pace with his stallion. Hyde Park was a crush of lords and ladies out to enjoy the fashionable hour. Everyone they passed acknowledged them with curious stares. It was little wonder, given the day's splendid weather and *tons* insatiable appetite for gossip.

A gentle breeze tousled Catherine's curls beneath her riding hat, and she felt a tiny thrill at being so near to Charles. Her conversation with Othelia ran through her mind as she gazed at him. She would speak with him today. She would tell him she had developed true feelings for him.

She nibbled her lower lip, searching for the

words. How did one tell their fake fiancé that they wanted more? What if he cast her away? He had told her from the beginning he did not wish to marry. Her courage wained at the thought.

Her confession could wait. She did not wish to spoil the afternoon. Instead, she gave a cheerful smile, then said, "Did you hear Louisa bested the Earl of Stone in a game of chess last night?"

"Indeed? That is quite an accomplishment," Charles replied, amusement ringing in his voice. "I would not have expected that from our dear Countess Stone."

Catherine laughed, real joy filling her at how Charles seemed to care for her family. "Oh, you underestimate my sister! She has always been a formidable opponent. And speaking of Louisa, she informed me the Duke and Duchess of Halloway will soon send invitations to the last ball of the season."

"Ah, the grand finale," Charles mused, his voice tinged with a hint of melancholy. "It seems only yesterday that the Season began, and now it is drawing to a close."

"Time moves rather fast when one is occupied with dances, dinners, and a fake engagement," Catherine teased, though her heart grew heavy at the thought of their time together drawing to an end. She would not think of it—not now. She pressed on. "Do you think Elizabeth will finally accept Lord Montague's attentions? I do believe he is smitten with her."

"Your youngest sister is certainly captivating," Charles admitted, a hint of a smile lifting the corners of his mouth. "As for Lord Montague, I cannot say. He may need to put forth more effort if he wishes to win her heart."

"True enough," Catherine sighed, thinking of her sister's insistence on true love. Her thoughts then turned to her cousin. "And what of Othelia? She seemed rather taken with the Earl of Southampton at dinner last night. I do wish she would give up mourning entirely. It has gone on far too long."

"Henry Thornton is a good man. I believe he would be an excellent match for Lady Othelia." Charles said, his tone thoughtful.

"Indeed," Catherine agreed, her mind spinning with the possibilities that lay ahead for each of them—and God willing, for herself and Charles. "So many lives intertwined, so many paths crossing... it makes one wonder what the future holds."

"Indeed, it does," Charles murmured, his gaze locked on Catherine's, his own emotions a stormy sea beneath the surface. For a moment, they shared a look that spoke volumes, their horses slowing to a gentle walk as the tension between them grew.

The last ball of the season loomed large in Catherine's mind, and though neither spoke further of it, she suspected it weighed on Charles too. They both knew their time together was fast running out. With every beat of their hearts, the bittersweet dance of their pretend courtship moved closer to its end. Did he question what would become of the fragile bond that had formed between them? Or were her feelings and desires one sided?

Perhaps she should confess before it was too late to do so.

Charles's smile faltered, his dark brow furrowing ever so slightly as he glanced away from Catherine. The muscles in his jaw clenched, betraying the tension that had seized him. His grip on the reins tightened, causing his steed to toss its head and whinny in protest.

"Charles?" Catherine asked, her voice laced with concern. She studied his face, noting the sudden change in his demeanor. "What is it? You seem... troubled."

Her pulse sped as she awaited his reply.

He hesitated for a moment before meeting her

gaze again, his dark eyes clouded with a mixture of anxiety and sadness. "I cannot help but worry about what will happen after the ball," he confessed, his voice barely audible above the rustling leaves and distant sounds of Hyde Park. "Our time together has been... more enjoyable than I ever imagined, and yet, its end draws near."

Catherine felt her heart constrict at his words, the truth of them hitting her like a blow. She, too, had been grappling with the reality her relationship with him would soon end, even as she allowed herself to be swept up in the dizzying whirlwind of emotions that accompanied their every encounter. But hearing Charles voice his concerns only intensified the ache within her chest. Perhaps he did share her feelings.

"Charles, I—" she began, struggling to find the right words, but he cut her off with a gentle shake of his head.

"Please, do not misunderstand me. I have treasured the time I have spent with you, and I am grateful for the chance to know you better. But we both knew from the beginning this was merely a pretense." He paused, swallowing hard as he continued, "I simply wish to ensure that when the time comes, we are both prepared."

Catherine nodded slowly, feeling tears prick at the corners of her eyes. She blinked them back, unwilling to let them fall. “I understand,” she murmured, her voice thick with emotion. “But know this, Charles, whatever the future holds, I shall never forget our time together.”

“Nor I,” he whispered, reaching out to briefly squeeze her hand."Let us find a more private place to discuss the details of your jilting me," he said, then urged his horse forward.

Catherine bit back the desire to say more, his increasing distance a silent reminder of the inevitable end to their passionate dance of deception.

Charles led their horses away from the main path, seeking a more secluded area of Hyde Park where they could continue their conversation.

They entered a clearing along the back of the park, and he dismounted. The sun shone down, sparkling off Catherine’s golden curls as he lifted her from her mount.

“Over there,” Catherine suggested, pointing to a

small area surrounded by tall trees and thick bushes. Charles nodded in agreement, his jaw clenched and his heart heavy with remorse. He wanted to refuse to end their engagement. He wanted to forget about the plan and take her to wife, but she had been clear about her wish to remain unwed. He cared too deeply for her to force her hand.

"Charles," she began, her voice shaking, "I know this is necessary, but I cannot help but feel... afraid."

He reached out, taking her hand and giving it a reassuring squeeze. "I understand, Catherine. Believe me, I will protect you. We simply need to stick to the plan."

Her gaze held his, the depths of her eyes revealing a vulnerability he had seldom seen in her. It touched him deeply, making him realize just how much she had come to mean to him during their time together. He would do anything to give her the life she longed for—even if it meant letting her go.

"Very well," she said, her voice a mere whisper. "What am I to do?"

Charles hesitated, then took a deep breath. "As we originally discussed, you will catch me with another woman in my arms and use my infidelity to jilt me. It is a perfectly respectable reason to cry off. One that will protect you from scorn and scandal."

Silence, punctuated only by the occasional call of a bird or rustle of leaves, surrounded them for long moments. Charles, noting the tension in Catherine's shoulders and the furrowed brow that spoke of her troubled thoughts, rushed to reassure her. "Society will focus on my roguish behavior and rally around you."

"Forgive me for my reticence," she eventually said, her voice laced with emotion. "I know we must discuss this matter if we are to be convincing." She glanced away, then said, "Please, share your plan, Charles. I trust you completely."

"Your faith in me means more than I can convey," he replied, his gaze searching hers. "We will want to ensure you catch me while most of the guests are still in attendance, but not so early on as to ruin the ball." Charles cleared his throat, not excited by the words he was about to say. "Our betrothal shall have a quick end," he said, his tone firm yet gentle. "When the hour nears midnight, you will enter the library to discover my liaison."

"And then?" Catherine asked cautiously, one brow arched.

"You will shriek, drawing attention to what is unfolding. The more witnesses we have the better.

You will need to show your anger and hurt. Yell at me and tell me you will not marry me."

Catherine hesitated, biting her lower lip as she considered his plan. "And what lucky lady will have her reputation ruined in order to save mine?"

"I will hire an actress and sneak her in through the terrace doors leading to the library. She will slip away during the aftermath. Nobody will know her, so she will not suffer for her part in the charade." While the idea of ending their engagement pained him, he knew it was what she wanted.

She took a deep breath before responding. "Very well. I believe it is a sound plan. I will give the performance of a lifetime. However, I must admit the thought of parting from you... it saddens me more than I believed it would."

Charles reached out and gently squeezed her hand as he searched her gaze. Her eyes filled with a mix of emotions. If he did not know better, he would say it was sadness and affection. However, he did know better and would not make a fool of himself by pretending otherwise. What he saw could be nothing more than friendship.

He forced a carefree grin. "The feeling is mutual, Catherine. It has been an honor and a pleasure to be engaged to you. Our friendship has been one of the most meaningful experiences of my life." He wrapped his arms around her and brought her close.

"Promise me something," Catherine said, her voice muffled against his chest.

"Anything."

"Promise me we will still be in each other's lives, even after all this."

He hesitated, knowing the danger such a promise held for his heart. But as he looked down at her pleading eyes, he knew he couldn't refuse her. "I promise, Catherine," he vowed, his voice thick with emotion. "No matter what, I will always be here for you."

"Thank you," she whispered, her voice shaking. "And I for you."

Charles took comfort in her words, for he would rather have her as a friend than not have her at all. Resisting the urge to take her mouth with his, he stepped back, releasing her. "Come now," he said softly. "Let us make the most of the time we have left. The last ball shall be here before we know it, and it will be a night to remember."

"Indeed," she said, forcing a small laugh.

He led her back to her horse.

A gentle breeze rustled through the trees as they rode back toward Rotten Row. The fashionable hour had passed and most of the lords and ladies had left the park for other amusements. Charles slowed his mount and looked at Catherine. "Shall we take our leave?" He asked.

"I fear we must," she replied, casting her glance toward her waiting groom.

They set their horses into a slow walk, deliberate, each hoofbeat carrying them closer to the end of their charade.

As they parted ways at the edge of the park, Charles felt the weight of their impending separation pressing down upon him. He watched as Catherine's shoulders slumped ever so slightly, her eyes downcast as she murmured her farewell. He raised her hand to his lips, planting a tender kiss upon her knuckles before releasing her.

"Until we meet again, Lady Catherine," he whispered, his voice thick with emotion.

"Until then, Your Grace," she replied, offering him a small smile before turning and riding away.

Charles watched her retreating figure until she disappeared from view. Then, with a heavy heart, he returned to his own residence, resigned to returning to his life the way it was before Catherine infiltrated it.

Gambling, women, and booze. Such debauched

things used to bring him great joy. Perhaps he would forget about her once he returned to his roguish ways.

Of course he would. After all, he was not the domesticated sort. All of this acting had simply messed with his brain affecting his better judgment.

Thirteen

The clock in Catherine's sitting room struck nine, its chimes echoing through the space like a haunting refrain. A shiver ran down her spine as she stood by the window, gazing out at the rapidly darkening sky. Charles had not called upon her today, and with each passing moment, her hope dwindled like the fading light.

"Curse him," she muttered under her breath, her fingers tightening around the delicate lace curtain. "Why must he choose tonight of all nights to stay away?"

"Perhaps he is simply preoccupied with his own thoughts," Othelia suggested gently, stepping up beside Catherine. "After all, tomorrow marks the end of your charade. It cannot be an easy prospect for either of you. I daresay he has feelings for you. I have seen the way he gazes at you. The way he treats you."

"He gave me every indication that he wishes for the charade to end." Catherine sighed, her eyes clouded with unshed tears. "I understand his wish to remain unwed, but I cannot bear the thought of our parting without... without having truly known him." She shook her head, her voice barely more than a whisper. "This may be my last chance to feel his touch, to taste his kiss—to know, even if only for one night, what it means to be truly, deeply loved."

"Then you must seize this opportunity, Catherine," Othelia insisted, her gaze steady and unwavering though her cheeks flamed red. "I cannot believe I am saying this, but go to him. Cast aside propriety and let your heart guide you. Tell him how you feel and take what you want."

Catherine nibbled her lower lip. The thought of such a bold move, both thrilling and terrifying. "But what of my reputation? If I were discovered..."

"Your secret shall remain safe with me," Othelia promised, her hand coming to rest on Catherine's shoulder. "As for everyone else, you must be carful. Wear a cloak and leave through the servants' entrance. Mind that you are not seen. I will cover for you with the family."

"Truly," Catherine breathed, the word heavy with meaning. "It is a reckless and bold thing to do, but I fear I will regret it for the rest of my life if I do not go to him this night."

"Then go," Othelia urged once more. "Do not let fear or doubt hold you back. Follow your heart, Catherine. You may discover that he loves you, too."

"He does not. Even if he does love me, he made it clear he does not wish to marry me." Catherine drew in a deep breath, her resolve hardening like steel in her chest. "But I have no wish to marry another. Before spending this time with Charles, I had no wish to marry at all. I will go to him, and I will make this night one neither of us shall ever forget. Then I will live on the memory for the rest of my days."

With determination burning in her eyes, she turned from the window and strode purposefully toward the door, her steps sure and unwavering. Tonight, she would throw caution to the wind and surrender herself fully to the man she loved. Consequences be damned.

Othelia grabbed Catherine's cloak and raced to catch up with her. "Wait," she whispered. "Put this on, and let me go ahead of you, so I can make sure the path is clear."

Catherine nodded, taking the heavy cloak and securing it over her, pulling the hood over her head to cast a shadow over her face. Once concealed, she followed behind Othelia, pausing at each turn to wait for Othelia to wave her forward until they reached the servants' exit.

She gave Othelia a mischievous smile as she slipped out into the night, her heart pounding against her ribcage like a wild, untamed beast. Come what may, she was going to Charles.

The evening air was cool against Catherine's flushed cheeks as she hurried through the dimly lit streets of Mayfair. Her heart pounded with a mix of fear and anticipation, and her breaths came in shallow gasps, visible in the moonlit night. She clutched her cloak tightly around her, the fabric whispering softly as it brushed against her silk gown. Her thoughts raced as fast as her footsteps, one question repeating itself like a mantra: Am I truly willing to lose my virtue for the sake of being with Charles?

The answer was both terrifying and exhilarating, a whispered truth that shook her to her very core: Yes. For the man she loved, she would risk everything—even her reputation and her place in society.

As she neared his residence, the gravity of her decision weighed heavily upon her. Her steps slowed, doubt gnawing at her insides. What if he did not feel the same way? What if their impending separation meant nothing to him? She might be about to make a complete cake of herself.

"Damn it all," she muttered under her breath, banishing the treacherous thoughts. She had come this far. She would not turn back now.

Taking a steadying breath, she raised her hand to knock on his door. The sound echoed through the quiet night, each rap feeling like a hammer blow to her fragile resolve. When the door opened, revealing Charles' handsome visage, she nearly faltered.

"Catherine," he exclaimed, stepping past his butler, surprise etched across his features. "What are you doing here? Is something amiss?"

"Charles," she whispered, tears threatening to spill over. "I needed to see you."

He threw the door wider, stepping aside, inviting her in. As she crossed the threshold, she knew there could be no going back. She was crossing more than just a physical boundary. This would have emotional repercussions as well.

Charles led her into a parlor and closed the door before turning to her. "Please, Catherine," he implored, his dark eyes searching hers. "Tell me why you have come."

"Because I love you," she confessed, her voice trembling with emotion. "And because I cannot bear the thought of spending the rest of my life without truly knowing you."

"Catherine," he stuttered, clearly caught off guard by her declaration. "I... I never meant for you to feel this way."

"Neither did I," she admitted, her hands twisting nervously in the folds of her gown. "But love cares not about ones intentions."

"No," he agreed softly, reaching out to cup her face in his hands. "It does not."

"Charles," she whispered, pressing closer to him, her heart swelling with the depth of her feelings. "I wish to spend this night with you. I know the consequences, but I am willing to face them if it means spending this night in your arms."

He stared at her for a long moment, his eyes filled with a mix of desire, warmth, and perhaps trepidation. Then, slowly, he leaned down to press a tender kiss upon her lips.

"Are you certain?" he asked, his breath warm against her cheek.

"I have never been more certain of anything," she replied, her resolve solidifying with each passing second. "Tonight, I give myself to you, Charles. In body and soul. Nothing need change between us. Only give me this night."

"Making love to you shall be my greatest honor," he murmured, folding her into his embrace. "You are in my blood, my lady. My heart."

As their lips met once more, sealing her fate, Catherine knew no matter what the future held, she would cherish this night for the rest of her days.

He swept her into his arms, then strode toward the stairway as she clutched his shoulders, peppering kisses across his jaw.

He carried her to his room, then laid her on the large four-post bed before coming down beside her.

In the dying candlelight, Catherine felt her pulse quicken as he gently pressed her down onto the softness of his bed. Their gazes locked, hearts beating in unison. He slowly undressed them both, each article of clothing discarded like a shell, leaving behind only the barest essence of their beings.

"Are you still certain?" Charles asked once more,

his voice laden with concern even as his body betrayed his desire.

"Yes, Charles. Make love to me," Catherine whispered, her gaze never leaving his. The shadows danced around them, casting an ethereal glow upon their entwined forms as they embarked on the most intimate of journeys.

Their lips met again, a fierce and passionate kiss that spoke volumes about the love that had been growing within Catherine, a love that was now reaching its crescendo. Charles trailed tender kisses along her neck, eliciting soft gasps from her as she clung to him, her hands tracing the contours of his muscular shoulders and back.

"Charles," she breathed, feeling the heat of his body pressing against her own. It was as if they were two halves of one soul, finally reunited after a lifetime apart. And though her heart broke at the thought of what tomorrow would bring, she knew this night would remain forever etched in her memory.

Their lovemaking was slow and sweet, an exploration of the deepest emotions that lay hidden within their hearts. He moved with a reverence that left her breathless, his touch gentle yet insistent as he sought to bring her pleasure. And when he finally entered her, it was as if the last barrier between them had crumbled, leaving only the purest form of love to bind them together.

As the hours slipped by, their bodies twined together as closely as their souls, she felt a peace unlike any she had ever known. She could not bear to think of the world beyond these walls. She would have gladly given her life for one more night in his arms, but she knew such a thing could never be.

As dawn approached, painting the sky in shades of rose and gold, they reluctantly untangled themselves from the cocoon they had woven. He helped her dress, his touch lingering on her skin as if he sought to memorize every last inch of her before they were forced to part.

"Stay with me," he whispered, his voice cracking with emotion. "Marry me, Catherine."

"Charles," she said, her voice soft and tears pricking at the corners of her eyes.

"I love you, Catherine. I have loved you for quite some time. Maybe from the beginning. I know you do not want to be beholden to a husband, but damnit, Catherine, I love you and you love me." he said, the pain in his voice cutting through her like a knife. "I want forever with you in my arms. By my side. In my bed. Say you will be mine for the rest of our days. That you will not leave and I will vow to support you in anything you wish to pursue. I will not cage you, darling."

"Perhaps not forever," she replied, giving a mischievous smile as her heart soared. "But for the rest of our lives."

Fourteen

The light of a pristine afternoon filtered through the stained glass windows of St. Paul's, Cathedral casting a kaleidoscope of colors onto the aged stone floor. The grand altar stood in quiet majesty, adorned with fragrant roses and lilies that perfumed the air. Anticipation hung thick in the church, while rows of guests sat upon polished wooden pews, their whispers intermingling with the delicate notes of the organ.

Lady Catherine nervously adjusted the orange blossom wreath on her head, her heart pounding with excitement and apprehension. Her family, gathered around her like a protective shield, offered reassuring smiles and gentle squeezes of her hands.

It was a moment she never dared dream of, and yet it felt more real than anything she had ever known.

"Deep breaths, dear sister," Louisa Mullens, Countess Stone, murmured, her green eyes shining with affection. The oldest of Catherine's siblings, Louisa, had always been her confidante - a hellion with her own ideas and a romantic outlook that often led to spirited debates between the two. Today, her light blond hair was pinned up elegantly, and a smile played on her lips as she looked at Catherine with pride.

"Thank you, Louisa," Catherine whispered back, squeezing her sister's hand gratefully.

"You are simply stunning today." Her youngest sister, Elizabeth, took her hands, her blue eyes shining with joy and blond hair pinned back in a romantic pile of curls. She grinned at Catherine. "I am so glad you found love."

Catherine squeezed her hands, smiling back. "You are next, dearest Elizabeth." She released her sister's hands and turned.

Catherine's brother, William, Duke of Thorne, stood tall and proud beside his wife, Olivia, near the door. As her guardians, they had guided Catherine with love and wisdom, shaping her into the woman she had become. William's blue-gray eyes shone with pride, while Olivia's amber ones gleamed with warmth. Their presence provided Catherine with a comforting sense of security.

"Remember, Catherine, we are here for you, always," William said softly, placing a hand on her shoulder.

"Indeed," Olivia chimed in, her voice gentle and soothing. "You are never alone."

Catherine's gaze then fell upon Othelia, who stood nearby in a lavender gown. Othelia's hazel eyes sparkled with happiness and shared secrets, and her dark hair seemed to glow in the soft light streaming through the windows. Her friendship had been a constant source of support for Catherine, especially during the most challenging moments of her life.

"Look at you," Othelia whispered, a hint of awe in her voice. "You are absolutely radiant."

"I owe my happiness to you."

"Nonsense." Othelia waved the words away. "I did nothing."

"You encouraged me to follow my heart. Gave me courage and guidance when I needed it. You are my best friend, Othelia."

"And you are mine." She straightened Catherine's sleeve. "Your betrothed awaits." She grinned.

William proffered his arm, and Catherine wrapped her hand around his elbow as the rest of the family moved to take their seats.

Her heart raced in her chest as she clutched her bouquet of delicate roses, their sweet fragrance doing little to calm her nerves. The hushed whispers of the gathered guests seemed to reverberate through the grand interior of St. Paul's, and as her eyes met Charles's, a wave of emotion washed over her.

As the hauntingly beautiful melody of the bridal march began, she took a tentative step forward, her gown rustling softly against the polished floor. The flickering candlelight danced upon the stained glass windows, casting vibrant hues upon the eager faces of their loved ones who filled the pews.

Charles stood at the altar, his attention never leaving hers as William escorted her toward him. His gaze filled with happiness, and a tender smile graced his lips, revealing the depths of his love for her. As she drew nearer, her chest swelled with pride, knowing she would soon be his wife.

"Who gives this woman to be married to this man?" the vicar asked, his voice steady and solemn.

"Her family and I do," William replied, releasing Catherine's arm and placing her hand into Charles's outstretched one. Their fingers intertwined, and the warmth of his touch wrapped around her. He was the gentleman for her. He loved her and supported her, and her love for him filled her with peace and joy.

The vicar led them through the traditional exchange of vows, each word heavy with meaning and love. As they spoke their promises to one another, the world around them seemed to fade away, leaving only the two of them in this sacred space.

"Your Grace, please take Lady Catherine's hand and repeat after me," instructed the vicar. "With this ring, I thee wed, and all my worldly goods I share with thee. In the name of the Father, and of the Son, and of the Holy Spirit. Amen."

His voice trembled with emotion as he repeated the words, slipping a simple gold band onto her finger, sealing their union. She marveled at the weight of it, knowing it symbolized his love and their promises to each other.

"Lady Catherine, repeat after me," prompted the vicar, a smile touching his lips.

Catherine took a deep breath and, with tears of joy pooling in her eyes, echoed the sacred words, "With this ring, I thee wed, and all my worldly goods

I share with thee. In the name of the Father, and of the Son, and of the Holy Spirit. Amen." Her hand shook ever so slightly as she placed the matching band on Charles's finger.

"By the power vested in me by God and the Church, I now pronounce you husband and wife," declared the vicar, his voice ringing out across the hallowed space.

Charles's eyes lit with mischief as he gently cupped her face, pulling her close for their first kiss as husband and wife. As their lips met, time seemed to stand still, and the love that had grown between them brought happy tears to her eyes.

When they finally broke apart, the room erupted in applause, the happiness of their loved ones reflecting the bliss that filled her own heart. She leaned closer to Charles and whispered, "Rogue."

He gave a cocky smile. "You would not have me any other way."

She could not contain her elation as he led her down the aisle and out of the church to their waiting carriage. This was by far the happiest day of her life.

The wedding party made its way to the grand hall of Catherine's family home. William and Olivia had spared no expense in hosting a splendid wedding breakfast for Charles and Catherine. The chandeliers overhead cast a soft glow on the ivory silk draperies and lush floral arrangements that adorned the tables.

Musicians played lively tunes and guests mingled animatedly, laughter ringing throughout the ballroom. In the center of it all stood Charles and Catherine, radiant with happiness, as they received heartfelt congratulations from their friends and family.

Tristin approached, his gate a bit unsteady as his leg was still mending. He came to a stop and leaned on his cain as he placed a hand on Charles's shoulder. "This is all my fault. If not for breaking my bloody leg..."

Charles chuckled. "Then we owe you and the reckless rider our deepest gratitude."

Tristin grinned, good humor shining in his blue gaze. "I knew you could not resist my sister's charms. You are a lucky man, Bedford. Treat her well."

"You have my word." Charles clapped his hand on Tristin's arm and the two men nodded.

Tristin embraced Catherine. "You know where to find me should the need ever arise."

"Thank you, Tristin," Catherine said.

As the guests took their seats, the sumptuous

feast began. Platters heaped with succulent roast beef, tender chicken, and fresh seafood were passed around, accompanied by steaming bowls of vegetables and fragrant sauces. Wine flowed freely, and the conversation grew ever more lively.

"May I have everyone's attention, please?" William, Duke of Thorne, stood up, raising his glass high. "I would like to propose a toast to my beloved sister and her new husband. Catherine, my dear, we have watched you grow from a spirited, curious girl into the strong and beautiful woman you are today. Charles, we welcome you into our family with open arms and hearts."

"Here's to a lifetime of love, laughter, and happiness for you both," Olivia added, her voice filled with emotion as she raised her own glass. "To the duke and Duchess of Bedford!"

"To the Duke and Duchess of Bedford!" echoed the guests, their voices filling the hall in unison.

As the wedding breakfast continued, the laughter and merriment only seemed to grow, reflecting the love and joy shared between Charles and Catherine.

And as they moved gracefully across the dance floor, hand in hand, gazes locked on one another, it was clear to everyone present that they were embarking on an incredible journey together—one filled with passion, adventure, and boundless love.

~

As the music faded, and the clinking of glasses signaled the end of the wedding breakfast, Charles and Catherine shared a knowing smile. It was time for them to begin their new life together, and they could not have been more eager to exchange the wedding celebration for time alone with one another.

"Shall we, my love?" Charles asked, extending his hand to Catherine, a roguish smile curving his lips.

"Indeed," she replied, her cheeks flushed as she placed her delicate hand in his strong grasp.

As they made their way toward the grand exit of the manor, their family and friends showered them with well-wishes and rose petals, creating a colorful cascade that seemed to mirror the joy and warmth swelling within Charles's heart. They paused at the threshold, turning to face each other, and Charles leaned down, capturing Catherine's lips in a passionate kiss that left no doubt about the intensity of his feelings.

"Is this real?" Catherine whispered against Charles's lips.

"Have no doubt, duchess," Charles murmured in response, brushing a stray curl from her forehead before leading her outside.

Hand in hand, they stepped into the waiting carriage, their eyes locked in a gaze that held a promise of devotion and desire that would last a lifetime.

As the carriage pulled away from the manor, the newlyweds journeyed toward a picturesque estate nestled in the lush English countryside. Surrounded by rolling hills and wildflower meadows.

"Welcome home, Duchess," Charles said softly, his voice filled with emotion as he helped Catherine down from the carriage.

"Home," she repeated, her eyes shimmering with unshed tears as she took in the idyllic scene before her. "It's more beautiful than I could have ever imagined, Charles."

"I am glad you like it, darling," he replied, the corners of his eyes crinkling with genuine affection. He wanted nothing more than to make her happy for the rest of their days.

As they entered the manor house, Charles delighted in Catherine's reaction. She walked slowly, taking it all in, eyes sparkling and lips curled into an ever-growing smile. They entered the drawing-room where rich mahogany furnishings contrasted beautifully with delicate lace curtains. A perfect blend of masculinity and femininity meant to keep them both comfortable. Fresh flowers had been brought in, and a fire crackled in the hearth, casting a warm, inviting glow over the room.

"Charles, this is simply perfect," Catherine breathed.

"You are free to make any changes you wish."

She shook her head. "I would not change a thing."

He followed her, his heart full to bursting with love and pride as she wandered from room to room, discovering surprises such as a library filled with her favorite novels and a garden blooming with fragrant roses.

"Your happiness is my greatest joy, Catherine," Charles said, wrapping his arms around her waist. They stood together, gazing out at the breathtaking view of the countryside, his heart beating with anticipation.

She turned, wrapping her arms around his neck. "In that case," she gave him a coy smile, "It has been far too long since you kissed your wife."

"Forgive me, wife," he murmured, his voice low

and husky. He leaned closer, his hand caressing her cheek with a lover's touch. "From this moment on, for the rest of our lives, I will indulge you with frequent kisses."

He brought his lips to hers, tenderly at first, before giving way to a hunger neither could deny. The taste of her was intoxicating. She had the faintest hint of vanilla lingering on her tongue, mingling with the sweet scent of the roses that surrounded them. As their mouths moved together, the texture of their lips became a dance of silk and velvet, a testament to the passion simmering beneath their carefully composed facades.

"Charles," Catherine murmured against his lips, her voice heavy with desire.

He tightened his arms around her waist, pulling her closer until not even a whisper could pass between them. "Sweet Catherine," he breathed, desire erupting within him. "I have longed for this moment, the freedom to taste your lips, to hold you close and know that you are mine."

"Then taste me, Charles," she urged, her own desire burning in her heated gaze. "Let us seal our vows."

"By God, you are exquisite," he groaned, his lips once more claiming hers with a fervor that left her breathless. Their bodies pressed together, the heat of their passion burning between them like a raging inferno.

"Charles," she gasped, her fingers finding purchase in the soft fabric of his coat as they kissed. "Promise me you will never let me go."

"Never," he vowed between heated kisses, their lips locked in a dance that spoke of love and desire, of promises made and hearts forever entwined.

Charles gazed tenderly at Catherine. With a firm but gentle grip around her waist, he effortlessly lifted her off the ground and carried her inside. This wonderful, beautiful, erotic creature was his duchess, his wife, his forever, and he was indeed the luckiest man alive. He loved her with every piece of himself and planned to worship her until she had no doubt how deep his love for her ran.

"Charles," she whispered with a catch in her breath, "you make me exceedingly happy."

He smiled softly, kicking the door shut behind them. "You deserve nothing less, my love," he murmured before lowering her onto the plush velvet chaise that occupied the corner of the room.

Charles knelt beside her, his fingers delicately undoing the ribbon that held her bonnet in place. As he removed the lace-trimmed accessory, a flush spread across her cheeks, belying her boldness. He continued to undress her with agonizing slowness. Each article of clothing peeled away like the petals of a blooming rose.

Charles' fingertips traced the length of her arm before deftly slipping the delicate gloves from her hands. The sensation of her warm skin against his own ignited a fire deep in his soul. He kissed her, slow and deep, then moved to unfasten her pearl necklace, planting soft kisses along her collarbone as he did so.

She closed her eyes, and small sounds of pleasure emitted from her as he trailed his lips across her silken skin.

"Charles, I…" she began, her voice trembling with vulnerability. "I have never known such love and tenderness as you bestow on me."

"Nor have I," he admitted, his breath hot against her ear as he gently removed her earrings. "And I promise to cherish and treasure you for all our days."

Tears pricked the corners of Catherine's eyes as she wrapped her arms around him, their hearts beating in time with one another. The last of her clothing was removed, leaving her bared to Charles in both body and soul.

"Beautiful," he whispered reverently, his hands grazing over her curves. "Absolutely beautiful."

"Charles," Catherine breathed.

"Sweet Catherine," he murmured, pressing a tender kiss to her forehead. "You have captured my heart completely, and I vow to protect and love you with every breath that I take."

Charles traced his fingers along the delicate curve of Catherine's collarbone, marveling at the warmth and softness beneath his touch. Her breath hitched as his hands continued their exploration, gently caressing her shoulders before traveling down her arms. Bloody hell, she was sweet. He would never grow tiered of her. Never get enough.

"Charles," she whispered, her voice wavering with desire. "I love you, too." Her eyelids fluttered closed, entrusting herself to his touch, as he continued to acquaint himself with every inch of her body.

"Your skin is like the finest silk," he murmured, his fingers now tracing the gentle swell of her breasts. The sound of their breathing filled the room, mingling with the scent of jasmine from Catherine's perfume. "I could spend an eternity discovering you."

"Then do," she pleaded, her heart racing beneath his touch. "Always."

He met her gaze, and it was as if they were connected by an invisible thread, one that pulled them closer until their lips met in a searing kiss. Their tongues danced together, exploring and tasting one another, as their bodies pressed closer.

"Tell me what you want," Charles whispered against her lips, his hand continuing its journey down her side, over her hip, and finally coming to rest on her thigh.

"I want to be yours, Charles. I want you to claim me." She breathed, her words laden with passion.

"I will never refuse you anything," he replied with a tender smile before carrying her to the bed.

The surrounding air grew thick with the heat of their passion, as he studied her body with his hands, lips, and tongue. They moved together in perfect harmony, each giving and taking, their bodies finding a rhythm all their own.

"Charles, oh Charles," Catherine cried out, her fingers digging into his shoulders as he thrust into her. He could feel the intensity of her love for him in every kiss, every touch, and every breath she took.

"My darling, Catherine" Charles panted, burying his face in her neck as he sought solace from the overwhelming sensations coursing through him. "I love you completely and irrevocably."

"I love you too," she gasped, as they clung to one another. Their cries of pleasure filled the room, wrapping them in a cocoon of passion.

As their lovemaking reached its peak, Charles and Catherine surrendered themselves to the moment, their bodies trembling with the force of their release.

Charles pulled her close, and she nuzzled her face against his chest as he played with a silken tendril of her hair.

The quiet symphony of their breaths intermingled with the rustling of the sheets as they lay in each other's arms, spent from their ardent lovemaking. The faint creaking of the bed beneath them seemed like a soft echo of their passion, as if it, too, had been swept up in the tempest of emotions that engulfed them.

"Charles," she whispered, as she feathered her fingers over his chest, "I never imagined… I didn't know it could be like this. Like it is between us."

"Neither did I," he confessed, his fingers tracing delicate patterns on her skin as they lay entwined, their hearts still racing from the intensity of their union. "But now that we know… I cannot imagine living without it. Without you."

His heart swelled with love for the woman he held so tenderly, her body responding to his every touch even as the echoes of their lovemaking began to ebb away.

She turned to face him, her eyes searching his—those deep pools of blue that seemed to hold all the sincerity and adoration he could ever hope for. "Promise me," she implored, her voice barely audible over the sound of their breathing, the wind outside gently tapping against the windowpane. "Promise me that no matter what happens, we will always find our way back to each other. We will always love each other."

"By my life, Catherine, I promise," he vowed, sealing his words with a gentle kiss on her lips. The taste of her lingered, as sweet as the most fragrant rose, and he knew in that moment he would do everything within his power to keep her by his side. Always.

"Charles?" Catherine murmured, her voice drowsy as sleep closed in on her.

"Sleep, my love," he whispered, brushing a stray curl from her forehead as he watched her drift off. "I will be here when you awaken, and every day thereafter."

He held her close, feeling the steady drumbeat of her heart against his chest. In this moment, with the woman he loved more deeply than he ever thought possible cradled in his arms, the world outside ceased to exist. All that remained were two souls bound by love, passion, and a promise that would transcend time.

Continue reading for an excerpt of the next book in Amanda Mariel's Fated for a Rogue series, *Rogue for the Taking*!

Prologue

Hertfordshire, England
Duke and Duchess of Thornes Garden Party

Othelia Grantham, Countess of Brighton, sipped her lemonade as she looked across the lush manicured lawn of the Duke and Duchess of Thrones country home. The ton had flocked to the duke and duchesses garden party and now dotted the landscape, enjoying refreshments, rowing in boats, and playing games. Sunshine washed the gently rolling hills surrounding the estate in warm light while birdsong filled the air. Most would call it a perfect afternoon.

Othelia considered it dreadful.

She had spent the previous two years mourning her husband, the Earl of Brighton, while becoming accustomed to being the widowed Countess of Brighton. She followed all the rules—not out of a deep love for her departed husband, though they had shared an affection of sorts, theirs was never a love match—she followed the rules out of respect for Lord Brighton and the vows they had exchanged.

For two long and tedious years, she had exemplified the picture of propriety, doing exactly what was expected of a widow and the daughter of an aristocrat. She'd had enough of mourning and propriety to last her a lifetime—more than enough, to be honest. She had been ready to start living after the required year of mourning. Only she lacked the courage. She feared upsetting her family, as well as Lord Brighton's siblings and the ramifications if she did.

And then there was her reputation to consider. Othelia had no wish to remarry, and because of her late husband's generosity, she did not need to marry again. In fact, he had left her a wealthy woman capable of providing for herself. But money could not keep one company and if she ruined her reputation, doors would surely be closed to her.

Still, she longed for adventure. For excitement and most of all for passion…

"Are you alright, Othelia?" Emma, Viscountess Linley, asked.

"You do seem a bit down," Othelia's cousin Louisa, Countess of Stone, added.

With a sigh, Othelia turned her attention to the ladies. "I was merely lost in thought. Contemplating my past and future."

"You have been widowed twice as long as you were wed. Do you wish to take another husband?" Louisa asked.

"No." Othelia wet her lips and glanced away. "But it is my fervent wish to start living. Most days I feel as if I perished on my wedding day. A situation that has only been compounded by my husband's death."

"This is all rather maudlin," Lady Covington said. "I was contemplating a stroll through the garden. Perhaps it would help clear your mind, Lady Brighton." She smiled at Othelia and stood. "Care to join me?"

Othelia did not know Lady Covington well. She had only met the lady on two other occasions, but she seemed to be a kind sort, and like Othelia, was a widow. Unlike her cousin Louisa and friend Emma, who were both happily married. She loved them dearly, but they could not understand Othelia, for they never suffered an arranged marriage void of passion and did not know what it was like to be a widow.

She returned Lady Covington's smile with a faint curve of her lips and nodded. "I should like that very much." Othelia stood, then strode toward the gardens with Lady Covington at her side.

As they entered the garden path, Lady Covington shot her a bemused glance. "I recognize something of myself in you. The way you speak of your life and the burning desire I see in your eyes. I suspect I know just the thing for you."

Othelia's brow furrowed. How could a woman who scarcely knew her presume to know so much? Still, Othelia could not ignore her curiosity and so she asked, "And what might that be?"

"I shouldn't like to put words in your mouth, Lady Brighton. But perhaps if you tell me what you are contemplating, I can be of assistance," Lady Covington said.

There was a warmth in the older lady's eyes that made Othelia trust her. "My marriage was arranged and my husband was considerably older than myself. We did not share a grand passion." She nibbled her lower lip and averted her gaze while gathering her courage. "I want to reclaim my life, to have friends who understand me and accept my choices, and I want to experience passion."

"But you do not wish to marry again?" Lady Covington arched one blonde eyebrow in question.

Othelia shook her head. "I do not wish to be under a man's control and there is no need, as my husband left me quite capable of providing for myself."

"Then I am correct in my assumptions. We do indeed have much in common. I choose not to remarry for the same reason and also suffered a loveless marriage." She reached for Othelia's arm. "I can help you. Come along," she said as she turned Othelia back toward the house.

"Where are we going?" Othelia asked, her curiosity at its boiling point.

"This is rather unconventional as meetings for new members are normally conducted at Lady Wyndam's home, or…" She waved a dismissive hand. "Never mind all that. I am taking you to speak with Lady Katherine Wyndam."

Othelia had met the lady in question shortly after her arrival at the garden party. She was aged with gray streaked hair and an ornate cane, but she radiated confidence. "I fear I do not understand," Othelia protested, digging in her heels.

"You will understand soon enough." Lady Covington said. "If you truly desire a support network and to reclaim your life on your own terms, then Lady Wyndam is just the person to help." Lady Covington started toward the terrace door.

Othelia stood in place waiting for the woman to say more. When it did not appear that she would, Othelia hurried to catch up. She had no notion of what she was getting herself into, but neither did she have anything to lose by speaking with Lady Wyndam.

Or did she?

There was no time to contemplate the matter as Lady Covington came to a stop before Lady Wyndham and announced, "May I present Lady Othelia Grantham, Countess of Brighton. She is a widow, not unlike ourselves, and I believe she would benefit from your guidance."

Lady Wyndham turned curious brown eyes to Othelia, then pointed her cane toward the chair across from her. "Do have a seat. I confess, I am eager to hear your story."

Othelia glanced at Lady Covington, who gave a firm nod before she lowered herself to the chair and met Lady Wyndham's curious gaze once more. She swallowed hard, discomfort rising within her as she attempted to determine the woman's meaning. What did the lady wish to know? And how would sharing private matters with this woman help Othelia? With a sigh, she said, "My story."

"Indeed. Tell me about your marriage, then we can take things from there." Lady Wyndham relaxed back against the gold brocade, her gaze remaining on Othelia. "I met Lord Brighton a time or two. Not that it is uncommon for an older gentleman to take a younger woman to wife, but I would wager he had decades on you."

"Four. He was forty years my senior."

Lady Wyndham's lips turned up in a satisfied grin. "I suspected as much. Now, do tell me your story."

"Ours was not a terrible match. Lord Brighton was kind and generous, but we did not share love..." Othelia collected her thoughts. She could scarcely believe she was telling her private affairs to a stranger.

Lady Wyndham leaned forward, offering encouragement. "It is alright, dear. You can trust us." She nodded toward Lady Covington.

Lady Covington tapped her finger on the arm of

her chair. "As I said, we are not all that different. You, me, and Lady Wyndham," she offered.

"Very well," Othelia said, then continued. "Our marriage was arranged out of necessity, as so many are. A lord and a lady who both stand to gain something. Lord Brighton desired a young wife capable of delivering a son. My family needed his money to save us all from ruin…"

Lady Wyndham listened intently as Ophelia conveyed the events of the previous three and a half years. At last Othelia said, "And now I find myself well past the mourning stage and ready to embrace a life of my own. I want friends who understand me, adventure and passion."

Lady Wyndham turned serious, her gaze sharp and lips pressed together as she studied Othelia. Then she asked, "You do not wish to remarry?"

"Certainly not," Othelia said, conviction ringing in her voice. "I wish to be my own master and keeper above all else. Though I have been considering a lover." Her cheeks burned at the admission and she averted her gaze to the aubusson rug beneath her feet. "You must think—"

"Nothing of the sort," Lady Wyndham tapped her cane against the door, effectively cutting Othelia off. "I think you understand your own mind and what you want. That makes you fortunate indeed." She leaned closer before continuing, "Further, I think you would make a wonderful addition to our widow's club. You need only agree to the rules and pay your dues."

"Widow's club." Othelia smiled. "What exactly are the rules?"

"Foremost, you must promise not to tell a soul about the club." Lady Covington pointed her silk fan at Othelia. "Do you vow to keep our confidence as we do yours?"

"You have my word." Othelia crossed her heart. "Your secret is safe with me."

Lady Wyndham stood, her cane tapping against the floor once again. "Then come along. We will tell you everything and collect your dues. Once that business is concluded, we will help find you a lover." She gave a conspiratorial nod. "I have a few rogues in mind I believe would serve you well."

Excitement filled Othelia as she followed the ladies from the parlor. Her life had changed, though she wasn't quite sure how. What she knew was that she'd forged an alliance with these women and suspected she would forever be grateful for them.

At the moment, she was elated, knowing that the rest of her story was just beginning.

Chapter 1

London, England
Ashbrook House, Mayfair

Alister Brinsley-Radclyffe, Duke of Ashbrook, swirled the liquor in his crystal tumbler as he stared at his brother, Benjamin, Lord Radcliffe. "Our situation has grown more dire."

"Do you mean your situation?" Benjamin said.

Alister took a long gulp of his brandy before returning his hard gaze to Benjamin. "Is it not I who pays your allowance?"

Benjamin nodded in confirmation before taking a swig of his own brandy.

"Then it stands to reason that we both have a problem. Without funds, I can no longer support you."

"You are not completely without coin." Benjamin moved to the desk and tapped his finger on the account ledger. "Surely there is something you can do."

"The creditors are growing more demanding, last years yields were half of what they once were. The country estate is near to crumbling." Alister sighed.

"Perhaps you can sell something. Mother's jewelry? Or some silver candlesticks." Benjamin turned toward the hearth. "There must be something left."

"Nothing that I am willing to part with."

"Then what are we to do?" Benjamin turned back to Alister.

Alister refilled his tumbler, splashing brandy over the side of the decanter. "We are going to have to tighten our spending until I can think of something else."

Benjamin sat his tumbler down with such force that it clanked against the wooden sideboard. "You could marry." He stalked toward Alister as he continued, "Find a rich heiress or a debutante with a large dowery."

"Do not think that I have not considered it. However, you know my thoughts on matrimony."

"Yes, well, desperate times and all that." Benjamin waved a dismissive hand. "No one said you had to love the chit. Just find a wealthy one and marry her. Problem solved."

Alister sank into a chair, stretching his legs out and letting his head fall back. "Why don't you do the marrying?"

"I am not the duke. Women will not toss themselves at me and fathers most certainly will not overlook my reputation to give their blessing." Benjamin leaned against the mantel, a grin tugging at one corner of his mouth. "Besides, you need an heir."

"I scarcely need one this instant." Alister tapped one finger on the side of his tumbler. "After being witness to our parents' damned union, I cannot stomach the idea of shackling myself. Though I admit a wealthy wife would be a damned good solution to our problem."

"Then it is settled. We will find you a wife with gold dripping from her reticule and coin overflowing her accounts."

"Do not get ahead of yourself. I nearly said it was

a good solution. Never did I agree to actually take a wife."

"Bloody stubborn, of you! Here we have the perfect fix to our problem and you are dragging your hessians rather than forging ahead and fixing this mess."

"Damn father for leaving us in such a situation to begin with." Alister drained his brandy in one long gulp. "If he would have paid half as much attention to our finances as he did mother's affairs and the gaming tables, we'd not be facing ruin."

"He loved her, you know," Benjamin said.

"He wanted to control her. Nothing more."

"Regardless, you need only do the opposite with your own wife." Benjamin moved to take the chair beside his brother. "Do not seek to control nor love your wife. Keep your attention on the estate and leave the gaming tables and vice to me."

"Yes, a marriage of pure convenience devoid of emotion and built on a solid understanding and mutual respect."

"That is what you have always said you would seek when the time came."

"And I have not changed my mind." Alister's jaw ticked with annoyance. "Do you believe there is a single debutante in all the world who would agree to such a match?"

"Not bloody likely." Benjamin shook his head. "But if I were a gambling sort," he chuckled, "and we know I am, I would wager there is a desperate wall-flower just waiting to be plucked or an aged spinster dreaming of a hero to sweep her out from under her father's roof."

"And how do you think ladies become wall-flowers and aging spinsters?" Alister asked, rising to fill his tumbler. With the task done, he turned and crossed his arms over his chest, giving Benjamin a hard stare. "Come now. You are never at a loss for words."

"I am attempting to devise a good argument."

"You cannot because there are only so many reasons for a woman to find herself in such situations. They are either scandalous, have notions of true love, do not have a substantial dowery, or have a displeasing continence. None of which will work for my future wife." Alister uncrossed his arms and reached for his tumbler. "I would like my wife to be my friend. She must be an excellent hostess and lady of the house. The lady must have a substantial amount of money and absolutely must be agreeable to a loveless marriage, yet trustworthy and committed to our union. I will not be cuckolded."

Benjamin sprang to his feet, his mouth curled up in a wide grin. "I've got it! You need to marry a widow."

"A widow?" Alister arched a questioning brow.

"Yes, a widow. Hear me out." Benjamin smoothed his cravat. "There are many young widows whose dearly departed husbands have left substantial sums of money, too. Further, they were married so they know how to run a house and their dispositions are well known. Most important for you, these young widows understand that marriage is a transaction. Find one who did not marry quite high enough the first time around and offer her the opportunity to become a duchess." He gave a satisfied smile. "Our little problem will disappear in no time."

Alister cleared his throat, as he searched for a suitable argument. In the end, all he could say was, "Our problem is not little."

"All the more reason for you to marry with all due haste."

Alister thought about the widows he had met and could not help but see his brother's point. There were a fair number of them that remained young. Many were without children, and certainly a handful of them were wealthy enough to get him out of his financial bind. There must be at least one among them who would be happy to form an alliance with him and agree to his terms. "We will attend the Hadley ball."

"And you will choose a wife?" Benjamin asked.

"We shall see."

Alister sat his empty tumbler on the sideboard, then left the room, Benjamin scowling after him.

CONTINUE READING

Get the next book in the Wayward Dukes' Alliance today!

Every Duke Has His Thorn by Angelina Jameson

A duke and a budding architect...

Nicholas Barton, Duke of Preston, returns to England upon the death of his mother, an overbearing woman who attempted to control the activities of her only child. After a disastrous month spent in London avoiding matchmaking mamas, the duke returns to his ancestral home, Barton Hall, in Lancashire. He finds the house rundown and the estate in shambles, thanks to a neglectful, greedy steward.

Miss Marina Davies, daughter of renowned architect Sir Robert Davies, has no time for the aristocracy. Her deceased mother was the daughter of an earl, cast off when she married a mere mister. Content to assist her father in refurbishing great houses, Marina isn't looking for romance, especially with a proud duke who left his responsibilities behind to travel the world.

Thrown together over several months, Marina comes to view the duke as a kindred spirit rather than an enemy, and Nicholas begins to realize that the strong young woman he'd seen as a thorn in his side is now the woman he wants as his wife.

About the Author

USA Today Bestselling author Amanda Mariel dreams of days gone by when life moved at a slower pace. She enjoys taking pen to paper and exploring historical time periods through her imagination and the written word. In her free time she can be found reading, crocheting, traveling, practicing her photography skills, or spending time with her family.

Visit www.amandamariel.com to learn more about Amanda and her books. Sign up for Amanda's newsletter while you are on her website to stay up-to-date on all things Amanda Mariel and receive a free eBook!

Amanda loves to hear from her fans! Email her at amanda@amandamariel.com or find her on social media:

Embark on an enchanting journey through the pages of the Fated for a Rogue series, a captivating collection of Regency historical romances that sweep you into a world of passion, elegance, and untamed desires. As societal norms clash with the yearnings of the heart, each novel unveils a tale of love that defies conventions and traverses the boundaries of class, circumstance, and expectation. From daring encounters at village May Day celebrations to the allure of Yuletide festivities, and from the unraveling of deceptive courtships to the pursuit of passion and reformation, the Fated for a Rogue series delves into the intricate dance between love and legacy, offering a vivid portrayal of romantic resilience against the backdrop of Regency England. Join us in exploring these captivating narratives where destiny weaves its threads through the lives of protagonists who dare to forge their own paths, leaving an indelible mark on the canvas of love and history.

Book 1: A Wallflower's Folly

Book 2: One Fateful May Day

Book 3: Fate Gave Me a Duke

Book 4: Earl of Stone

Book 5: Who Needs a Duke

Book 6: Rogue for the Taking

Thank you so much for taking the time to read *WHO NEEDS A DUKE.*

Your opinion matters!

Please take a moment to review this book on your favorite review site and share your opinion with fellow readers.

Milton Keynes UK
Ingram Content Group UK Ltd.
UKHW010845101023
430299UK00004B/205

9 798215 240861